NOTES FROM THE FIELD

NOTES FROM
THE FIELD

Angela Ahn

WITH ILLUSTRATIONS BY JULIE KWON

tundra

TEXT COPYRIGHT © 2021 BY ANGELA AHN
ILLUSTRATIONS COPYRIGHT © 2021 BY JULIE KWON

Tundra Books, an imprint of Penguin Random House Canada Young Readers,
a division of Penguin Random House of Canada Limited

LIBRARY AND ARCHIVES CANADA CATALOGUING IN PUBLICATION

Title: Peter Lee's notes from the field / Angela Ahn; Julie Kwon,
illustrator.
Names: Ahn, Angela, author. | Kwon, Julie, illustrator.
Identifiers: Canadiana (print) 20200182315 | Canadiana
(ebook) 20200182331 | ISBN 9780735268241 (hardcover) |
ISBN 9780735268258 (EPUB)
Subjects: LCGFT: Novels.
Classification: LCC PS8601.H6 P48 2021 | DDC jC813/.6—dc23

Published simultaneously in the United States of America
by Tundra Books of Northern New York,
an imprint of Penguin Random House Canada Young Readers,
a division of Penguin Random House of Canada Limited

LIBRARY OF CONGRESS CONTROL NUMBER: 2020933319

Edited by Lynne Missen
Designed by John Martz
Printed and bound in Canada

www.penguinrandomhouse.ca

1 2 3 4 5   25 24 23 22 21

Penguin
Random House
tundra   TUNDRA BOOKS

THIS NOTEBOOK IS PROPERTY OF:

PETER LEE

Chapter 1

MAY THE FORCE
BE WITH YOU

TUESDAY, MAY 14, LUNCH

CONDITIONS: LIGHT RAIN, HIGH HUMIDITY

The ball came at me so fast I barely had time to throw my right hand up in the air to block it. But just like Deinocheirus, a dinosaur from the late Cretaceous period, I have unusually long arms. The leather of the ball grazed my gloved fingertips. I had just counteracted a basic scientific law: the ball would have stayed in motion and sailed right through the goalpost if I hadn't applied the smallest amount of force. Force wreaks havoc on motion, and in this case, it caused the ball to change its trajectory, leading to the sweetest sound a goalie can hear—*thunk*. The ball firmly hit the goalpost and rebounded back into play. That was a close one.

"No!" Ryan Gagnon screamed as he clenched his fists and arched his back in frustration. "You got lucky, Peter!"

He clearly did not understand physics at all. Luck has no part in science.

We glared at each other briefly and then Ryan ran ahead to keep close to the action.

I leaned against my goalpost and watched the other boys run back to the far end of the field. It wasn't long before they stopped to argue.

"I did not!" Ryan shouted.

"I saw it, Ryan! You're lying!" Joe Flores threw his hands up. "It was so totally a handball!" Joe was my good buddy and an excellent judge of character.

The rain was starting to come down, but we never called games off because of the weather. Sometimes I walked around with wet shoes all day and didn't notice until I got home and peeled my socks off—instead of toes, I had stinky prunes.

It looked like the argument was going to be a while, so I ripped off my goalie gloves and patted my front pant pockets. I felt the familiar lumps of my small coil notebook in my left pocket and my inhaler in my right pocket. My asthma was getting better the older I got—I hadn't even had to go to the emergency room in a few years—but I was still supposed to take a dose every day and an extra dose *before* exercise, not *during* exercise. Sometimes, like today,

I forgot to follow the plan. I made sure it was a good time to turn my back to the game so I could privately take a quick puff.

The game had come to a complete stop. Even if he had touched the ball, Ryan would never admit it. Joe was trying to argue, but this was *Ryan*. I sighed and waited for the game to resume. I needed to keep loose, so I swung my long arms around and around like helicopter blades. As a goalie, the only player on the field who can use their arms, all this height has an advantage. At five foot nine, I'm the tallest boy in my fifth-grade class. I get to stand in the middle of the back row for the class photo. That's the Top Dog spot and it has been mine for years.

I am really freaky-tall if you factor in the Korean thing. The Korean thing being that I'm a Canadian-born Korean. Koreans are known for lots of things: electronics, cheap cars with a weird company name, addictive TV shows and K-pop; but Koreans aren't known for their height. I break all the rules.

As the argument got more heated, I watched Samuel Pak leave his basketball game and casually saunter up to Ryan and the other boys. Samuel and his friends in sixth and seventh grade played basketball on the court right next to the end of the soccer field.

As soon as they saw Samuel coming, Joe and Ryan stopped arguing. They stood frozen, waiting in anticipation for Samuel to speak. If a person could be so cool that it left everybody else feeling chilled, that was Samuel.

Samuel was the only other Korean boy in the whole school and sometimes we saw each other at family parties because his grandmother was friends with Hammy, my grandmother, and he would always be polite, but just not overly talkative. It was the same at school. He had this quiet bad-boy vibe about him, like you wouldn't be totally surprised to see him sitting in the principal's office because he either got in trouble or because he was helping with something. He was hard to figure sometimes. I mean, he wasn't my *friend*, but he didn't treat me like carrion either. From the other end of the soccer pitch, Samuel gave me his usual chin-up greeting, which I returned.

I couldn't hear everything Samuel was saying, but I did catch: "Who cares, dudes? Get a life and just *play*. This ain't the World Cup." Samuel sounded disgusted. He flicked his hand through the air, dismissing them.

When Samuel spoke, fifth graders listened. He said his piece and slowly walked back to the basketball court. He wiped his forehead with the back of his hand. Even when he was sweaty, it wasn't gross, it was athletic.

I held on to the goalpost for balance to stretch out my calf, while watching the argument get sorted out. When they stopped talking, I jumped to the center of the goal. I put my goalie gloves back on and assumed my "ready" stance.

"Game's on!" Liam shouted down the field to me. Liam and I had only one thing in common—our last names. Liam was also a Lee, but he was the Chinese kind, not the Korean kind. He was Ryan's best friend. Was it a coincidence that they were both like two tiny, barky attack dogs? I doubt it.

Joe was running across the field, dribbling the ball between his feet. He was speedy and had good control of the ball. His Vancouver Canucks shirt was a blur of blue and green as he danced around the field, looking downfield for an open player. Ryan started to charge at him, trying to take possession of the ball from Joe. Ryan had intense, angry eyes, which was kind of just his everyday look.

Joe was having none of that. He kicked the ball so hard that Ryan barely had time to get out of the way. It ricocheted off Ryan's backside—kinetic energy at its best. I couldn't stop the "Ha!" that came out of my mouth. His pale gray track pants were left with a dirty, wet circular stain. Right on his butt. He'd have to walk around like that all day. It was perfect. I saw a lopsided smile flash across Joe's face. That stain was going to make Ryan even madder. The ball rolled out of the soccer field and bounced toward the playground, closer to the school.

Because the rain had started to come down hard, the playground was empty, except for L.B. I eyed my little sister from across the field. No matter the weather, she was *always* in the playground, even if she was alone. She was usually alone anyway.

The boys cupped their hands around their mouths and shouted, "L.B.!" They pointed to the ball.

My little sister had been whizzing back and forth on the zipline. When she reached the end of the line, she gracefully jumped onto the platform and skipped to the ball, which had come to a stop near her.

L.B. picked up the ball and balanced it in her right hand. She looked like a baseball pitcher at the ready—her body turned to the side, her elbow bent and then her high leg kick. The ball flew through the air in an impossibly long arc.

"Whoa," said Liam. His cheeks were flushed and his dark hair shiny with sweat. I watched him as he watched the ball fly through the air.

"Thanks!" the other boys shouted across the field as the ball landed near their feet.

"Hi, Petey!" she yelled, waving. I shooed her away. The game was back on.

Unlike me, L.B. was small. She was the smallest child in her second-grade class. She sat in the front row on the end of the bench in her class photo. That's the Shrimp Spot. Nobody wants the Shrimp Spot. In this year's class photo, L.B. wore yellow leggings with a unicorn pattern all over them, and a white T-shirt covered in rainbows. Her socks even had pink hearts; you could see the pattern poking out between her running shoes and the hem of her pants. She always dressed herself in a way that made her look . . . I don't know . . . kind of loud and flashy, like an exploding glitter bomb. Sometimes all the girl stuff on her clothes was a bit much. Even the rain jacket she was wearing right now was covered with sparkly bits. She was hard to miss.

As Ryan ran by me, he said in his mocking squeaky voice, "Hi, *Petey!*" I tried to swat at his back with my gloved hand, but I missed. He didn't have a younger sibling who humiliated him like I did. I had a love-hate thing with Ryan. I loved to hate him.

The bell rang and, as I half-jogged, half-walked back to class, I heard the supervision aide blow her whistle and yell at L.B., like she does almost every day. "Last one in again, L.B.? Get back to class!"

Chapter 2

FULL S.T.E.A.M. AHEAD

"We've got to go in thirty minutes," Mom said as she glanced up at the clock in the kitchen. She passed me a bowl of oatmeal. I rubbed my head and tried to open my sleepy eyes wider.

"Why?" I perked up.

"We're going to the . . ." Mom squinted and stared at her note on the calendar. "Chemical Engineering Lab of Innovation."

I sat up straighter. "That sounds cool!"

Dad snapped his newspaper open and, without looking at me, said, "Oh, sorry, Peter. It's not for you."

I slumped over my breakfast. Of course not. Why would it be for me?

I listlessly shoveled a spoonful of oatmeal into my mouth and squished it around before swallowing.

L.B. skipped into the kitchen, still wearing her pajamas with emoji faces all over them, and she pulled out a chair.

"Good morning!" L.B. said happily to nobody in particular.

Mom pointed a finger at her. "We've got that thing today."

L.B.'s shoulders slouched slightly. "Is that today?"

"Yes. It's a real privilege." Dad pushed his glasses up on his nose and folded the newspaper closed. He took a sip of coffee. L.B. sighed and looked outside. She flipped one of her braids behind her shoulder.

"Do I have to go?" I asked as I scraped my last spoonful of oatmeal from the bowl. The weekends were my "Ryan-free" days and I usually managed to do something relaxing, like watch dinosaur videos, or sometimes I'd call Joe and we'd go to the corner store and get a freezie. Taking L.B. to a new program was not exactly as fun as sucking brightly colored sugar water out of a plastic tube.

"Yes," Mom answered decisively as she sat down at the table.

"Can't I just go to Hammy and Haji's?" I put my bowl and spoon into the dishwasher.

"They're coming too."

"I love extended family outings!" L.B. said as she nibbled her breakfast.

"You don't have much time, so *please* try to eat quickly!" Mom said firmly to L.B. Last month, it took her four hours to eat half a pomegranate.

"Why are Haji and Hammy coming?" I asked.

But before Mom could answer, there was a knock at the door.

"That's probably them," Mom said. "Peter?" She motioned with her head toward the door. I looked at Dad. He wasn't about to move either. They were experiencing the scientific phenomenon known as inertia: a body at rest tends to stay at rest. Inertia was the scientific word for laziness.

I was still wearing my dinosaur pajamas, the ones covered in different-colored Triceratops on skateboards, not the pair with the big Diplodocus across the chest, but it was just Hammy and Haji, and they had seen me in my pajamas a thousand times. When I opened the door, I was startled because it was *not* Hammy and Haji. It was a brown-uniformed delivery man wearing a baseball hat. I tried hiding behind the front door.

"Special Saturday delivery!" He handed me a stack of

envelopes and turned to go back to his van. "Cool pj's."
He winked at me.

"Thanks," I replied reluctantly, closing the door. I
hated it when I couldn't tell if an adult was making fun of
me or not.

I looked at the top envelope, which was addressed to
Mom. The sender was Golden Sunset Active Living Centre.
I stared at it for a few seconds trying to figure out why Mom
would be getting special delivery mail from a place like that.

"Peter, it wasn't Hammy and Haji?" Mom shouted
from the kitchen as she leaned back in her chair so she could
see me standing in front of the doorway.

"No, it was a mail delivery." I held up the envelopes to
show her.

"Mail delivery?" she asked, surprised.

I started to say, "The Golden Sunset . . . ," but she leaped
out of her seat, managing to put the coffee cup down at
lightning-fast speed, and grabbed the envelopes out of my
hand before I could look at the next one. Until that very
moment, I would never have described my mother as fast
and agile, but caffeine has amazing powers on adults.

"What—" I started to say. My hands were in midair,
imagining that they were still holding on to the envelopes
that had just been there a second ago.

"It's probably just junk mail," Dad said casually as Mom dashed upstairs with the envelopes. "We've got to get going soon! You should brush your hair, your teeth! Lots of things need brushing!" He laughed strangely.

I squinted at him suspiciously.

There was another knock at the door.

"*That* will be Hammy and Haji!" Dad said as I turned the knob.

"Good morning, everybody!" Hammy said as she stepped in and gave me a warm hug. She was wearing a colorful floral scarf and a yellow cardigan sweater—it was her signature look. She had countless scarves and every color of cardigan. She always wore some combination of the two. Her hair was short and she had given up coloring it a long time ago. I loved how her hair had different shades of gray and some black hairs that had refused to age.

"Peter!" Haji gave my back a gentle pat.

L.B. hugged Hammy, then turned to Haji and did a little leap, springing herself at him. He caught her, but barely.

"L.B.!" Dad chided. "You've got to make sure he's ready when you do that!" She shrugged her shoulders unapologetically.

Haji laughed. "No problem. I got her!" L.B. climbed off him and brought his pants down a little in the process. He hitched them up. He liked his pants a little baggier and higher than most people would wear them. Not quite to his armpits, but close.

Mom came downstairs dressed in a crisp white button-down shirt and black trousers. Her big thick hair gave off the smell of hair spray. She handed Dad a sport coat and then clapped her hands together twice. "L.B.! Peter! Upstairs! Change your clothes right now! We don't want to be late!"

9:55 A.M.

It was taking forever to find the right classroom. "Can I play *Asteroid Cataclysm* on your phone?" I asked Mom. It was a game where you launched asteroids toward the Earth to try to create conditions that cause a mass dinosaur extinction.

She sighed. "But we're almost there, Peter."

"Come on. Just a few minutes! I'm so bored. Why am I here anyway?"

When half her face does this sideways pucker, I know she wants to say no but doesn't really have a good reason to.

"I suppose it's all right, but just for a few minutes and keep the volume down. As soon as we get there, give it back," she said as she dug around the inside of her purse and passed me the phone. "Try not to crash into anything as we're walking."

Eagerly, I grabbed it out of her hand. A few minutes of game time was better than zero minutes. I was sure I could launch at least two asteroids by the time we found the classroom.

"Big building!" Haji commented as we walked down the hallway, our footsteps echoing loudly.

"Easy to get lost in here!" Hammy agreed.

Ever since L.B.'s kindergarten teacher recommended she go for some tests, my parents made her do stuff like this. They called it her "enrichment" activities.

"Are you excited to meet your new mentor?" Dad asked her as we approached the classroom. He pushed up his glasses on his nose.

L.B. shrugged her shoulders. "I'd rather be playing," she confessed. "It's such a nice day." She launched herself into a cartwheel in the middle of the hallway.

"L.B.! Not here!" Dad scolded, looking around to make sure nobody had seen.

"Playing is a waste of your potential!" Mom said.

L.B. frowned and lightly skipped down the hallway instead.

"This is it." Mom stopped in front of the last door in the

14

hallway, and before she knocked, she patted her hair into place. "L.B., I wish you'd worn something less . . . sparkly."

L.B. looked down at the shiny rhinestone-studded apple on her shirt and sighed. When Mom tapped L.B.'s arm and motioned for her to straighten her posture, L.B. put out a big smile and straightened her back just in time to greet Dr. Esther Stephanova, director of the Chemical Engineering Lab of Innovation.

"Good morning!" Dr. Stephanova put out her hand for L.B.

"Good morning!" L.B. said with a confident handshake.

"Hi," Mom said enthusiastically. "We're the parents." She pointed. "Grandparents, brother." She stuck her hand out and I gave her back the phone. I had managed to play only one level, but Earth was well on its way to destruction.

I stared inside the classroom and felt my face start to feel twitchy. Why did L.B. get to do all the cool stuff? The class was set up like a working laboratory. The large center table was clearly Dr. Stephanova's work space. The surface of the table was covered with test tubes, petri dishes and a whole assortment of jars containing brightly colored powders. I was struck by the display on the back wall of the room. "How many Erlenmeyer flasks do you have?" I blurted out. My voice was louder than I wanted it to be.

Every member of my family turned to look at me.

"How do you know the name of those *thingies?*" Dad asked, pointing his finger at the wall of flasks.

"You can actually learn things from YouTube, you know," I replied, a little miffed.

Dr. Stephanova looked at me, surprised. "Well, young man. Most people just call them conical flasks and don't know that they were named after the German chemist—"

"Emil Erlenmeyer." I finished her sentence for her.

She smiled at me. "I collect them. These flasks are my own personal collection. I believe the oldest one here is from approximately 1920. I would love to get a nineteenth-century one . . . one day! Are you a chemist?"

"Me?" I asked. "No, paleontology is my real passion, but I read an article—"

"Anyway . . ." Mom cleared her throat loudly and looked at her watch.

"Oh yes, we should get to it, shouldn't we?" Dr. Stephanova said. "Will you all be staying?" She looked directly at me. Her white lab coat was buttoned up neatly. I stared at her name, embroidered onto the pocket, which was full of pens. Even if she hadn't been wearing a lab coat, she just *looked* like a scientist—medium-brown hair pulled off her face, wire- framed glasses. She seemed serious and professional.

"No, not him. Let's focus on L.B. We're here because this is her Girls in Science scholarship, after all!" Mom said quickly.

"Some boys like science too," I grumbled to myself.

"Dad and I are going to stay, just for the first session. If that's okay, Dr. Stephanova?"

"Of course!"

"We brought work to do, so we won't be in the way." Mom pulled out a few files from her bag. "I can hardly keep up with all these mortgage applications!" She chuckled to herself and laid the papers on a table in the corner, away from Dr. Stephanova's main work area.

Mom stared at Dad in a way that made it pretty clear that he was supposed to talk now.

"Oh yes, I brought . . . some work to do too," he mumbled. Dad worked at the Burnaby School District in the International Education Office and, unlike Mom, carried no papers. He felt his pockets, retrieved his phone and stared at it intently.

"Right. I have something for you, L.B." Dr. Stephanova reached into a built-in closet behind the main table in her lab.

She pulled out a little lab coat and held it up for L.B. And just like her jacket, L.B.'s was personalized. The letters

L and *B* were embroidered in a fancy script font in black thread. L.B. perked up and turned her back to Dr. Stephanova, held out her arms to get help putting the jacket on and then smoothed the lapels down. Her small hands lingered over her embroidered name.

"What a treat!" L.B. said. "Thank you so much."

"You are very welcome," Dr. Stephanova said kindly.

Looking around at the lab and then seeing L.B. in that monogrammed lab coat made my brain shake. My breathing became ragged and I tapped my right pant pocket.

Mom turned to Hammy and Haji, opened her eyes extra wide and stuck her neck out like a chicken. When that didn't work, she tried talking in a loud voice.

"Mom! You said you had something you wanted to take Peter to see?"

"Oh, oh, right!" Hammy said, startled.

"Okay. Good. We'll be done at . . . ?" Mom stared at Dr. Stephanova.

"Let's start with one hour today. But the following weeks may be a bit longer. Depends on what fun projects L.B. and I get started on."

"Okay, meet us back here then," Mom said as L.B. raised her hand to wave goodbye. Hammy and Haji did the same. I couldn't even force myself to say anything as simple as "bye." It just wouldn't come out. Mom ushered us out of the room and closed the door.

I was trying hard to pretend I was okay. It wasn't L.B.'s fault, but sometimes things were just so unfair. I listened to my footsteps echoing in the empty halls to relax and tried to use sheer will to push down all the stomach acids rising through my esophagus. Hammy reached for my hand and held it firmly as we silently exited the building.

We strolled down East Mall, a pedestrian boulevard on the campus of the University of British Columbia, where all the science buildings were located. Modern glass buildings stood right next to buildings made of stone blocks and covered in ivy that had been carefully clipped. Looking at all the building names made me feel better. I could feel myself calming down.

My favorite building name had to be the Advanced Materials and Process Engineering Lab. What on Earth did they study in there? Whatever it was, it *had* to be amazing. It felt pretty cool to be surrounded by all this *knowledge*, old discoveries and new revelations happening inside these very buildings. I imagined one day I'd have an office in a building like one of these.

Hammy stopped and pulled out a newspaper from her large brown leather handbag. She read it carefully. Haji peered over her shoulder. "I know where that is." He patted her shoulder.

"Where are we going?" I asked Hammy.

She showed me the newspaper. "There's a free art show at the Student Union Building."

I stared at her blankly.

"Free student art show?" I mean, art was okay, but not exactly how I wanted to spend my morning.

She glared at me. "What's wrong with that?"

"Ah, it's free. What else we gonna do now, eh, Peter?" Haji said with a soft chuckle. He adjusted the fit of his baseball hat. It was the one he usually wore, with the Canadian and Korean flags intertwined.

"Maybe we see the work of the next great Canadian artist!" Hammy said. "Come on. We only have one hour."

Hammy tightened the knot of her scarf and then wrapped her arm through mine so we were walking with our elbows locked. She started humming a song I didn't recognize, and as she walked, she looked up at the trees and I could tell she was happy to feel the warm sun on her face and to just be here walking down the boulevard. It was hard to stay upset with Hammy, or anything, when she looked like that.

Chapter 3

FACT: SISTERS ARE ANNOYING

When the bell rang, I grabbed my backpack and raced to the Big Rock. It was an igneous rock, possibly granite. I guesstimated that this rock was at least 140 million years old. I mean, that was just a guess. I'm not a geologist. The most important thing about the Big Rock was that you couldn't miss it. Located right near the front doors of the school, it made a very handy meeting spot.

When I started kindergarten, Mom took me to and from school the first day, but she couldn't do it after that because she had to work. So when Hammy and Haji took over picking me up at the end of the day, she told all three of us, "Go to the Big Rock! Don't forget!" All these years later, it's still where we meet every day.

Hammy and Haji waved when they saw me coming from around the side of the building. I wasn't sprinting, but jogging at a good clip. Suddenly I got jumped from behind and crashed to the ground. My backpack went flying off my shoulder and landed three feet away. Now I knew what it felt like to be on the receiving end of a headbutt from a Pachycephalosaurus.

As I lay awkwardly on my side, the wind knocked out of me, I stared up at my sister's face, smiling right at me. I pushed her off.

"Sorry! I thought you knew I was coming!" She looked like she was ready to burst out into loud giggles, the laugh that sounded like a series of exploding firecrackers.

I sat up, hugged my knees and tried to catch my breath. My inhaler and my coil notebook had fallen out of my pockets, so I picked them up quickly and went to retrieve my backpack, still partially doubled over.

Hammy and Haji had hurried over to me.

"Peter! You okay?" Hammy asked as she tilted her head to try to look at me.

"Yeah, yeah, Hammy. I'm okay." I brushed my knees off and glared at L.B. "You have *got* to stop doing that!"

As Ryan walked by, I heard him say to Liam, "Looks

like Peter can't even walk without tripping over his own giant flipper feet!"

I took a slow breath and tried to ignore him.

"L.B., remember, you need to warn people," Haji scolded.

"Sorry," she said sheepishly. She then held out her backpack for Haji to take and ran toward the Big Rock. She liked to launch herself over it in different ways—feet together, right foot first, left foot first, hands together, right hand first, left hand first. One day she was going to try headfirst and then she'd be sorry.

"That girl has too much energy!" Haji laughed as he tossed L.B.'s tiny purple backpack over his shoulder.

"You're telling me." I swiped at the dirt on my pants.

We started to walk home. Hammy grabbed L.B.'s hand and they swung their arms back and forth in big, exaggerated swings. Haji and I walked behind them like regular dudes, just walking. At the first intersection, Hammy stopped suddenly, even though it was clear of cars. Her eyes scanned left and right.

"What's wrong, Hammy?" L.B. asked.

Hammy let go of L.B.'s hand and brought her right hand to her face. "Which way?" Hammy asked, her eyebrows scrunched.

"Hammy, the usual way." L.B. pointed straight ahead.

"Oh." Hammy laughed at herself. "I just forgot."

"Silly Hammy!" L.B. grabbed her arm and hugged it. "We have been walking this way for *years*! We could all probably make our way home blindfolded!" She paused. "In fact, I think I might try that next time."

3:30 P.M.

We walked into their house, put down our things, slid off our shoes and I gave the picture its usual adjustment.

"You going to say it again, Peter?" Haji's eyes twinkled as he dropped his keys on the front table.

"Every time I'm here!"

"When are you going to take this thing down, Haji?" We both said it at the same time in a robotic tone of voice. It was our in-joke.

The "thing" was a *Time* magazine cover from 1987 with a headline that read "Those Asian-American Whiz Kids" in a bright yellow font, framed and hanging limply on the wall directly across from the front door. Haji told me that he and Hammy had immigrated to Canada in 1981, when Mom was very young. It was the first time he had seen an Asian face on the cover of a magazine, showing regular Asian kids,

24

so he thought it was a really important picture. Before that, he didn't even know faces like ours could be on a magazine cover. To him, this picture was so important that he framed it. But now, I mean, I know it's sentimental to him, but really, the picture just looks kind of cringey and so dated. I wished it could go inside a nice dark box deep in his crawl space, so he could keep the memory but not put it on display.

"You say what you like about Haji's picture, but don't talk about taking down *my* favorite picture!" Hammy laughed as she took the photo of my family off the piano and hugged it. "I never get rid of this!"

"But, Hammy," I said, raising my finger to give everybody a cue. In unison, all four of us said, "It's the world's ugliest family photo."

It was a picture of my parents, L.B. and me. It's hard to believe, but it is even more cringey than the *Time* picture. Last year, we got a coupon in the mail from a new photography studio that opened up down the street. "Special Introductory Offer!" it said. Dad scheduled an appointment. When we got there, we discovered it was actually a Vietnamese sandwich shop with a white photography screen in the back.

The owner, Minh, made us sandwiches and took our picture—not exactly at the same time, but almost.

We probably should have eaten the banh mi sandwiches *after* the picture, because my mom, who usually looks awkward in photos anyway, had cilantro in her teeth. It wasn't a huge piece, but it's definitely there. And Dad had little white dandruff flakes on his glasses, even though he swears they're bread crumbs from the crusty French baguettes. I was going through my big growth spurt, so I'm all limbs. Also, I'm blinking. I blink in approximately 57 percent of all photos. This one included. About every other year, I blink in the school class photo too. It's uncanny. L.B., on the other hand, is smiling perfectly for the camera, her hair braided and pinned neatly with a bow. With her hand resting on her left hip, she looks adorable. It's disgusting.

Hammy stared lovingly at the picture before she put it back on the lace embroidery that covered the top of her piano. "L.B.'s so cute here." She tapped the photo as if she was giving L.B.'s cheek an affectionate swipe. One day, I was going to sneak that picture into the backyard and bury it in my excavation pit. I'd leave it as an artifact for future generations to unearth. Also, that way, I wouldn't ever have to look at it again.

"Haji, I have online homework from my math tutor. Can I borrow your computer?" L.B. asked.

"Of course!" He stood up to turn it on. The computer

was so old it would take about ten minutes to boot up.

I looked out the window. "It's nice outside. I think I'll do some digging," I said.

"Need help?" L.B. asked.

"Sure." I shrugged reluctantly. "Not so hard this time! It took me almost thirty minutes to find the femur last time."

She smiled mischievously. "Do you think dinosaurs left flags in mud pits to announce the location of their bodies for paleontologists to find them easily millions of years later?"

I rolled my eyes and pointed to the back door. "Just go."

L.B. dashed through the kitchen, slid open the door and ran to the backyard. She did a somersault, leaped up, grabbed the lowest branch of the Japanese maple tree and swung off of it. She snatched the mesh bag full of bones hanging off the hook nailed into the side of the garage. They weren't real fossils; they weren't even real bones, just plastic replicas. It didn't matter because this was purely for practice. She started digging with one of the shovels Haji always left outside for us.

My excavation pit wasn't much to look at—it was basically a large hole in the ground that Haji had filled with sand. But this pit was where I was learning to become a paleontologist. I had to cover it up with a piece of fitted plywood when I wasn't using it. I learned that the hard way.

The neighborhood raccoons didn't know it was the field study area of a burgeoning scientist; they thought it was their local latrine.

We watched L.B. from the kitchen, and she yelled, "No peeking!"

This back corner of Hammy and Haji's yard was all mine. It used to be where Hammy had a vegetable garden, but a few years ago, she said she was getting too tired to keep it up.

"Ah, I'm glad you still use the pit," Haji said.

"Why wouldn't I?"

"Sometimes kids lose interest in things after some time."

"Don't worry. I still love it."

"Good." Haji nodded.

"Haji? Um, do you think we could make some improvements?" I motioned to the pit outside.

"Sure! What do you have in mind?"

I went to my backpack and pulled out *Fossil Dreams: A Young Scientist's Essential Guide.* This was my favorite book of all time. My parents bought it for me for my birthday only last year, but I had read it so much the corners were fraying. I had the page marked with a bright orange sticky note.

"I think I need one of these." I showed him a picture of a grid that paleontologists use over an active dig. It's useful for mapping out exactly where bones are located in the ground. He read the description carefully. There are lots of different versions, but usually they involve a wooden frame with metal wires spaced every six inches squared.

"No problem. We can do for a weekend project soon, okay?"

"Thanks, Haji." I smiled.

"You want snack before you dig?" Hammy asked. "L.B.'s not done yet anyway." She had taken off her scarf and cardigan. It was a warm afternoon and she opened a window.

"Always!" I answered. You don't get to be this tall by not eating at every opportunity.

Hammy shuffled into the kitchen, opened the fridge and began to wash some fruit. She got out an old knife from her kitchen drawer and began to slice. I sat at the table and waited.

She held out a plate of cut-up fruit. Her apple slices were always perfectly even and fanned out across the plate, and instead of cantaloupe cubes, she always used a melon baller and put a toothpick in each ball. Sometimes she arranged them in a pyramid.

I grabbed a few apples and said, "Thanks!"

I chewed my fruit while I watched L.B. She was hunched over the pit, walking around it quickly and doing some final rearranging. She stood up, cocked her head to the side, and when she patted down the sand with the back of the shovel, I knew she was finished. L.B. looked up and saw me watching her. She smiled and waved.

I went to get my *Field Notes and Observations* journal from my backpack and said to Hammy, "I'll be in the backyard if you need me."

5:10 P.M.

"How was your dig?" Mom asked me when I came back inside. She was sitting next to L.B. at Haji's computer, still in her work clothes.

"Good!" I replied. "The dust didn't bother me today. I added a bit more water to keep the dirt wetter." Dust usually didn't affect me too badly, especially if I remembered to use my inhaler in the morning.

"Calcium chloride and magnesium chloride are used as commercial dust suppressants. A superior choice to water, actually, because they stay moist," L.B. shouted from the computer. Dr. Stephanova probably taught her that.

"Probably not great to touch with my *bare hands*," I retorted.

L.B. glared at me sideways before she took off her giant headphones and said, "I found something very interesting!"

"Hmm?" Mom said.

"You know how we've discussed a road trip as our summer holiday?" L.B. asked.

"Yeah," I said.

"Did you know the Royal Tyrrell Museum offers educational programming?" L.B. asked.

The greatest dinosaur museum in Canada. I had been wanting to visit this place for years and of course I knew from their website that they offered programs, but what good does it do a kid in Vancouver when the museum is all the way over in Alberta?

"Educational?" Mom perked up.

"Yes, look here." L.B. pointed to the screen. "A Junior Scientist Dig!" Mom concentrated on the screen. My heart started to beat faster.

"They will take you out to a real fossil site!" Mom said, turning to me with her eyes wide open.

My chest tightened at the thought of me at a real fossil site.

"Huh!" Mom leaned back in her chair and looked like she was thinking hard. "You know, your dad and I had talked about maybe driving to Banff or something for summer holidays. The museum's in Drumheller, which is—"

"Only 251 kilometers, or approximately 156 miles, from Banff. It's merely two and a half hours of extra driving," explained L.B.

Mom leaned in to look at the map on L.B.'s screen. "Flip back to the museum site," she instructed L.B., and she scanned the page again. "Peter, this program sounds absolutely perfect for you! Practical, real-life scientific inquiry!"

I leaned in to look at the screen too. *Junior Scientist Dig: Hands-On Paleontology. See a real active fossil site. Dig for real fossils with paleontologists from the Royal Tyrrell Museum.*

"So, Peter, should we do it? Make a vacation out of it and sign you up for this program?"

I nodded silently. My heart was pumping so hard my ribs were sore. The wobbly feeling in my legs forced me to sit down.

"Unfortunately, L.B., you aren't old enough to join Peter," Mom said, frowning. I tried not to smile. There was nothing *unfortunate* about that at all.

"That's okay," L.B. replied, shrugging.

"Peter, let's sign you up! There's only one spot left in one of the afternoon programs on July 4. We'd better grab it," Mom said, and L.B. began typing, filling in the online form.

"Last step. Payment." L.B. held out her hand and waited for Mom to open her wallet.

"I guess I'd better book time off work and tell your dad to do the same," Mom said, pulling out her credit card. "We have to get some accommodations arranged too."

"On it!" L.B. started typing furiously.

It was all coming together so quickly I almost couldn't believe it. Me, in Drumheller . . . it was going to happen!

"Hammy and Haji will want to come too," L.B. reminded Mom.

"Of course."

"Hammy! Haji!" L.B. yelled from her seat. "We're going on a road trip!"

They shuffled in from the kitchen. Hammy wiped her hands on a kitchen towel.

"Road trip?" Hammy asked.

"I need to check my calendar. So busy, you know," Haji joked.

"You're retired, Haji!" L.B. laughed. "You've got loads of time."

"Okay, you just tell us when. We'll follow." Haji grinned.

"This will please you, Petey! You get a free subscription to their newsletter when you sign up for a program." L.B. turned her head to look at me as she pointed at the screen.

A grin erupted on my face. My cheeks hurt, the smile was so big. I looked at Mom, L.B., Haji and Hammy, and I was just so excited I almost forgot to breathe. Even though it was still more than a month away, I just had this feeling that this was going to be the best summer of my life.

Chapter 4

ORIGIN OF THE SPECIES (L.B.)

THURSDAY, JUNE 6, 11:15 A.M. (T-MINUS 26 DAYS
BEFORE HOLIDAYS!)
CONDITIONS: DRY, WARM BREEZE. HIGH CLOUD

Our hotel rooms were booked and the trip to Drumheller
was officially on. The only problem was there were still more
than three weeks of school left. Dragging myself to school
each day was getting harder and harder. It is no secret that
nothing useful happens in school in June. As we all sat
at our desks, our restless legs kept twitching, aching to get
outside. Everybody was dreaming about long, lazy summer days when parents forced kids to wear thick layers of
sunscreen and everybody either smelled really good (like
Hawaiian coconuts) or really bad (like a sweaty body in
need of a shower).

Mr. Costa didn't get the memo. He always made us
do silent reading after morning recess and today was no

different in his mind. People had their books propped open, the bottom edges of the spines resting on their desks, and while it looked like people were reading, if you listened, you could tell that nobody turned any pages. I looked over at Joe. His eyes had glazed over and his book slipped out of his hand.

I was trying to focus, but it was hard even for me, and I was reading something I was interested in! The Royal Tyrrell newsletter had come yesterday and I was trying to concentrate on the article about new techniques for more accurately aging fossils, but I lost my focus and started flipping through the pages. The back page caught my eye.

IT'S CONTEST TIME!

Attention, all kids! The next quarterly newsletter will be all about kids and dinosaurs!

If you're reading this newsletter, you are probably a dinosaur enthusiast. Show us why you love dinosaurs!

We are accepting all kinds of work: short essays, pictures, whatever you want. The only criteria? Dinosaur related—obviously!

RULES FOR SUBMISSION

1. All work must be done by children aged twelve or younger. Parents, hands off! Let the kids do it.
2. Work must be received by **October 1** to be eligible.

Please send all entries to the attention of Kendra at the Royal Tyrrell Museum. We look forward to all your submissions, but only work suitable for the upcoming issue will be selected for publication.

I stared at that back page for a long time.

Ryan stretched and leaned back in his seat. He whispered, "Hey, Petey, what kind of nerd magazine are you reading?"

I glared over at him and held his gaze for a few seconds before I turned back to my newsletter. He looked over at Liam and they smirked together.

When the timer, set for twenty minutes, buzzed, we put our reading material away and I took one final look at the back page of the newsletter, making sure I remembered all the details, before I put it away. Then Mr. Costa stood up, smoothed his button-down shirt and grabbed a pile of paper.

He handed out our new assignments. The first people to see the paper started to moan and complain. "Another writing assignment?"

Even though there was rumbling and whining, Mr. Costa just ignored it. He cleared his throat and started his boring explanation. "To conclude our unit on narrative writing, I want you to write a paragraph between 250 and 400 words. The topic is 'What I Hope to Become.'"

"Everybody knows what Peter is going to write about!" Ryan shouted. "Look! He was even reading a magazine about dinosaurs." Before I could react, he quickly got out of his seat, reached into my desk, pulled out my newsletter and waved it around.

Ryan flipped his long bangs while he threw in a giant eye roll. He had a very specific haircut. It was buzzed around most of his head, but he left his dirty-blond bangs long on purpose. They looked like windshield wipers for his eyes.

The class chuckled. I felt my face get warm and I shot him an evil look.

"Well, you *have* been obsessed with dinosaurs since kindergarten," Stephanie Aquino agreed. She tossed her long, dark hair over her shoulder. If Ryan hadn't been the most annoying kid in the class, Stephanie would have gladly accepted the job.

"Try preschool!" Liam said. I glared over at him. I could still see the sweat on his scalp from recess.

I casually put my hand over my dinosaur eraser to hide

it. Then I tried desperately to remember if I'd worn my dinosaur socks. I pushed the hems of my track pants down with my feet, just in case.

"Huh, they're having a contest. How very interesting," Ryan said, looking at the back page. He broke up the word *interesting* into four very distinct, slowly articulated syllables, just how any other evil dictator would have said it.

"Give it back now!" I yelled, and I used my long arms to snatch it back. His arms were stubby like the tyrannosaur branch of dinosaurs and he was no match for me in a grabbing contest. Once I had it back, I carefully ran my hand over the pages to get out any creases and put it back in my desk.

"Ryan, Peter, that's enough," Mr. Costa warned. "Class, Peter has a passion. We should all be so lucky to have something we truly love to do." He looked up wistfully. "I think having something to work toward is fantastic." I was going to ask Mom to buy Mr. Costa a really good year-end gift, not just a Starbucks gift card.

"Whatever! It's like a child's hobby that he should have outgrown by now," Ryan said. He scoffed, flipping his bangs again.

I couldn't hold it back anymore. I yelled, "It's a hard science! You probably don't even know how to spell *paleontology*!" I glared at Ryan.

"P-A-L-E-O-N-T-O-L-O-G-Y," Ryan said smugly. Even though I could see only one eye through his bangs, I could tell he was completely satisfied. There was a ripple of chatter throughout the class. "I'm the son of a journalist, remember? I spell and write better than everybody in this room. It's in my DNA. I'm going to be a journalist too! That's an *important* job dealing with current issues, not old, irrelevant dinosaur bones."

Was being a total jerk-bag in his DNA too? Suddenly the room felt extra hot.

"Hey," Joe whispered to me, casually leaning sideways in his chair. "You look like a cooked lobster. Don't let him get to you." I gave him a slight nod and tried to calm the rage.

The sail connecting the back vertebrae of the Spinosaurus was thought to regulate its body temperature. Right now, I wished my ears did the same thing; instead, they felt like two torches stuck to the side of my head.

Mr. Costa cleared his throat and raised his voice. "Anyway," he said as he tried to get control of the class. "I don't think it's appropriate to dismiss other people's dreams. Let's be respectful of our different interests and goals." He stared at Ryan, who stared right back. "You need only be worried about yourself and your own assignment."

Mr. Costa glared around the class to make sure every-body was listening.

"Here's something you might want to know. Your assign-ment is due tomorrow, so I'd use the next thirty minutes to get writing. Remember how I feel about working indepen-dently and doing the best you can do!" Mr. Costa said.

Tomorrow! He wasn't letting up one bit. I changed my mind. Maybe a Starbucks gift card was good enough for him. I tried to settle down and to think about what to write. My chest was starting to feel tight, but I was not about to let Ryan see me wheeze, not now of all times. I closed my eyes and tried to control my breathing.

I ran my hand over the sheet of lined paper to feel its smoothness and wrote "My Future in Paleontology" across the top. I drew some interlocking femur bones around the margins. A piece of paper and a pencil in my hands always made me feel better.

"I might just enter a little something into your precious dinosaur museum contest, just because I know whatever I enter will be ten times better than whatever *you* do," Ryan whispered as he walked behind my chair, using the pretense of needing to use the pencil sharpener.

My nostrils flared, but I remembered Joe's advice and remained calm, pretending I didn't hear him. Everybody in class settled down to work. The only sounds were Ryan cranking his pencil into a sharp spear and my blood simmering.

I put down my pencil and pulled my small notebook out of my left pocket. Pushing out the tiny pencil I had tucked inside the coil, I simply wrote the word *Ryan*. I drew a face with devil horns and stupid bangs. **PAYBACK: WHEN I WIN THE ROYAL TYRRELL CONTEST.** I tucked my tiny pencil back into the coil and quietly put my notebook back in my pocket while trying to suppress a grin.

There was a knock at the door. I glanced up and saw Samuel, delivering a note. A few girls in the class giggled and whispered to each other when they saw him. The boys straightened their backs, even Ryan.

Even though Samuel and I knew each other better than most people realized, I still got the feeling that he thought I was a bit of a nerd, or maybe it was that—compared to him—I just felt like one. Samuel saw me in the room and gave me a chin-up greeting.

Mr. Costa quickly read the note and put it down. "Peter, go with Samuel to the office. They need your help."

"But it's almost lunchtime!" I protested.

Mr. Costa walked up to me and whispered in my ear. "It's about your sister."

11:40 A.M.

Our walk to the office was silent. "I was there to help with lunch announcements and they asked me to get you," Samuel finally said as he pointed to the first-aid room.

L.B. was alone, sitting slouched over on the little bed in the corner.

"Thanks, Samuel," I replied.

"She's calmed down a bit but, man, she was craze-balls earlier," he whispered. He went behind the counter and set up the microphone for announcements. "Good luck, dude."

I stepped into the first-aid room and L.B. perked up when she saw me.

"L.B., what's going on?" I could hear Samuel's voice over the crackling PA system, telling students about picking up their yearbooks next week.

"Ms. Tarkas! She had her baby early!" L.B. said. "She assured me she would finish the school year. Statistically, it was only an 11 percent chance that she would have her first child before thirty-five weeks of gestation. I hate it when statistics disappoint me!"

"What are you, a doctor or an eight-year-old?"

"Petey, there's an ill-prepared substitute teacher!"

Oh. Now I knew *exactly* where she was going. L.B. had, what my mom told me to call, "quirks." She had to have her hair in a braid. She ate slowly—really slowly. She talked like an old lady who had read too many novels. And her biggest quirk of all: she absolutely hated her real name.

"She keeps calling me Charlotte," L.B. cried. Nobody dared use her real name—except ill-prepared substitute teachers.

"Did you tell her?"

"Petey," she said with an edge of impatience and disgust. "Of course I did. But she can't seem to comprehend basic information!"

"Do you want me to talk to her?"

"Desperately." She frowned, her eyes sad.

The principal, Ms. Broadbent, popped her head in the room. "All better now, L.B.?" She had a singsong voice, like a bird chirping.

"Petey's going to make it better."

Ms. Broadbent put her hand gently on my shoulder and mouthed, *Thank you!* I would have hoped she—as a professional educator—wouldn't leave it up to a ten-year-old to sort out an eight-year-old's problems, but then again, this was no average eight-year-old.

I held out my hand for L.B. to take and she squeezed it tightly as we walked down the hall to the primary wing. She gripped my torso fiercely as we neared her class and I knocked on the door. The lunch bell had already rung, and people were buzzing around packing up their lunches and getting ready to go outside.

"Charlotte," the substitute teacher said as she noticed us by the door. L.B. erupted in tears.

"Uh, Ms. . . . ." I glanced up at her name written in thick red dry-erase marker on the board. "Francis," I said. She

waited for me to continue. "Can I talk to you about . . .
Charlotte?" I whispered the name.

"Sure," she said, looking at me attentively.

I stepped inside the empty classroom and said, "You
can't call her that."

"Call who what?"

I pointed to L.B. "That name. She hates it."

"Charlotte?"

"Sh!" I said. L.B. exploded with fresh tears. "She likes
L.B. Didn't Ms. Tarkas leave a note about it or something?"

"Elby?" Ms. Francis said, confused. "E-L-B-Y? I
couldn't figure out what everybody was talking about."

"No, like the letter *L* and the letter *B*."

"I'm the Little Beast! Don't you see?" L.B. wailed, and
she dropped to the floor on her knees.

"It's kind of a long story—you don't need to hear it," I
started to tell Ms. Francis while I tried not to get too caught
up in L.B.'s melodramatic show.

"She must know my origin story!" L.B. yelled.

"Please, I'd love to know her origin story." Ms. Francis
looked intrigued.

"Okay, okay." I waved my hand impatiently. I took a
breath and prepared to tell her how it all began. "L.B. used to

climb up my body. She still does. I'm tall, right?" I waited for acknowledgment.

Ms. Francis nodded and said slowly, "She *climbed up* your body?"

"It was annoying, so I got mad once when she was doing it and yelled to my parents, 'Get this Little Beast off of me'—or something like that. She thought it was funny." I looked down at her.

"It *is* funny!" L.B. said from the floor.

"For a while, she actually insisted we call her Little Beast." I stared at L.B. and a tiny smile emerged as if she was remembering those days fondly. "But Little Beast is kind of . . . weird, right? So we settled on L.B. for short."

"It was a compromise!" L.B. sniffled. "Is it so hard to comprehend?"

"L.B. . . . ," Ms. Francis said slowly, nodding. Her eyebrows scrunched into a tight knot. I could see her trying to put all the pieces together. "Okay. I think I got it now. Is that what she was trying to explain earlier? Ah, I see. No more Char—that other name."

"Now we understand each other perfectly," L.B. said as she wiped her eyes and smiled. She stood up and hugged my waist.

Even though she came home from the hospital with a bracelet that said "Charlotte Ji Eun Lee," it's best to use L.B.

I looked at L.B. "Can I go eat lunch now?" My stomach grumbled and the only thing I could think about was the roast beef sandwich waiting for me in my lunch box.

Chapter 5

HANDS-ON LEARNING

Haji, Dad and I loaded the wood into the minivan, but we still had some shopping to do. We got the store clerk to cut strips of pressure-treated lumber into pieces long enough to make my grid. They even mitered the corners for us in a perfect forty-five degree angle so all we had to do when we got home was screw the corners together into a square joint. Dad and Haji said they could put it together, no problem. It was like constructing a picture frame. But we weren't done. We headed back inside to find the right wire to complete the grid.

Dad told a sales clerk, "We need some wire."

"What kind of wire?" Dan was wearing a bright orange apron that had a "Fifteen Years of Service" badge pinned to his front pouch. I felt confident Dan could help us.

49

"For a . . ." Dad looked at me for help.

"A paleontology field excavation grid," I said quickly. "It's going to be four by five feet, and we need wire that is rustproof."

"Ah, what you need is galvanized wire. Aisle twenty-eight. Follow me."

Dan led us a mile into the cavernous store, with building materials piled high up to the ceiling, and then pointed to the selection of wire on the shelf. "Lightweight, medium-weight or heavyweight?"

I said "heavyweight" at the exact moment Haji said "medium-weight" and Dad said "lightweight."

We all laughed. "Medium is a good compromise," Dan wisely suggested. He pulled down a roll and passed it to me. "It comes in rolls of fifty feet. Is that going to be enough?"

I looked at Dad, who looked at Haji, who looked at me.

"Oh, I wish L.B. were here," Dad said as he pulled out his cell phone and tapped his calculator app. For once, I agreed with him.

"I'll leave you to it, then," Dan said. "Good luck with your grid."

"Thank you!" I said, holding up the roll of wire.

Dad looked up from his phone. "Actually, this is a great math problem for you, Peter! You have a grid that is four feet long by five feet wide. If we place the wires every six inches, how much wire will you need?"

He was the one with the calculator in his hands! I had *not* come to the lumber store to do extra math homework.

"Just buy two rolls," Haji said impatiently.

"Peter can figure it out!" Dad said encouragingly.

"I already figured it out. Buy two." Haji grabbed a second roll.

"You should let Peter use math to solve real-life problems," Dad said seriously to Haji. "It's what we in the education field call 'hands-on learning.'"

"Standing in lumber store tapping on calculator is not hands-on. *Building* is hands-on!" Haji started walking down the aisle, smirking.

2:20 P.M.

"You can take car," Haji said to Hammy as she and L.B. were getting ready to go. We had just come back from the lumber store and had moved the last piece of wood to the backyard.

"No, I don't feel like driving," Hammy said. "We'll take the bus."

"If you don't keep driving, you feel too nervous to drive and then you never drive again," Haji warned.

"But I usually have my chauffeur!" Hammy said, pointing at Haji.

Haji waved his hand through the air and said, "Okay, okay. Have a good time. Don't buy too much . . . stuff."

Hammy tied her scarf around her neck and stared at him wickedly.

"Hammy only buys *treasures*, Haji," L.B. said.

"Why do all her treasures look like pigs?" Haji said as he pointed at the corner cabinet in the living room. Through the glass front you could see it was crammed full of all the ceramic pigs Hammy had collected over the years. Haji was right. She could call them "treasures," but it was still basically used junk, usually in the shape of a pig.

Hammy and L.B. giggled.

"You sure you don't want to come treasure hunting today, Peter?" Hammy teased as she put on her shoes.

I had been treasure hunting with her and L.B. exactly one time. I will never go again. On that day, I realized shopping can cause some people, namely me, physical and emotional suffering. Hammy and L.B. had spent *two straight hours* walking up and down every single aisle of every single antique store on Main Street, touching every old piece of junk previously owned by a person who was now dead and probably haunting the store that had their old stuff.

"Look at this!" Hammy would say, holding up an object. Then she and L.B. would stand there and discuss its artistic qualities. *Nice detail. Colors are so attractive. Shape so pretty.* I wished I had taken an extra puff on my inhaler before we had started shopping. The smell, the dust and the idea of all this stuff that used to be owned by people who were now *dead* really creeped me out and caused my lungs to rebel every time we walked into a different store. Then, when it seemed they would end the day empty-handed, they finally found a ceramic pig. They both became ridiculous.

"Hammy!" L.B. shouted. She held the "treasure" up in the air for Hammy to see.

Hammy quickly shuffled to L.B., trying to avoid banging her hip into all the old furniture. Her eyes were bright and shiny.

"L.B.! You found one!" she said breathlessly.

Then she made a noise I've never heard before. It sounded like a pig squealing.

L.B. copied the noise and they both stood there, clutching the ceramic pig between their hands. Then they started jumping up and down in the middle of the store, squealing.

I hid behind a grandfather clock and pretended I wasn't with them.

"Ha, ha, Hammy," I said now. "You know how I feel about treasure hunting."

"I know, I know. Just kidding. You have very important work to do with Haji." I nodded.

"Lock door behind us, okay? Don't want anybody to steal Haji's favorite picture." Hammy winked as she nodded her head toward the *Time* cover.

I waved goodbye and closed the door. As usual, the picture frame slid and I automatically straightened it out.

"Come, Peter! Time to build!" Haji held his power drill in his hand and gave the trigger two pumps—*Rrrrr! Rrrrr!*

"Before we get started, I think there's still a little math problem that needs solving!" Dad reminded me.

I sighed. Dad didn't ever give up. Mom was out shopping, but I knew that if she had been here, she would have agreed with Dad. In this family, it's hard to avoid extra math.

"*Cha*, you take your job in education too serious sometimes." Haji shook his head.

"I need paper," I said, suppressing my frustration.

Dad hovered over me while I calculated.

"There, eighty feet," I told him as I showed him my work. Turns out Haji's guess in the store was right, and we needed only two rolls if we were placing the wire every six inches.

He adjusted his glasses as he scrutinized my numbers. "That number looks correct. So let's recalculate. What if we put the wire every *four* inches instead?"

"Why would we do that?" I questioned.

"Just for fun!"

"Why you think math problems always fun?" Haji said. "*Cha*, let's just build this thing." Haji drilled the pilot holes for the screws and then let me use the drill to put the screws in. We all helped wind the wires around the screws to tighten them into place. When my grid was finally done, it looked exactly like the one in my book. I think we were all pretty happy with the end product. I couldn't wait to use it next time I did a practice excavation.

"Anything cold to drink, Haji?" I asked as I peered inside his refrigerator. We had worked mostly in the shade, but the day had been hot.

"There's some cold barley tea," he told me as he wiped his forehead with a paper towel.

"Pour me some too, Peter!" Dad gasped. He was the sweatiest out of the three of us. "That took longer than I thought." He went to the sink to splash water on his face.

"Probably because you insisted on turning it into a 'fun' hands-on math problem," I muttered with my face inside the fridge.

As I took a nice long drink, Hammy and L.B. opened the front door, hands full of shopping bags. "Hello! We're home!"

I walked up to them in the living room. "Find anything good?"

Hammy smiled broadly at me. "Today was the best day, wasn't it, L.B.?"

L.B. started jumping up and down as if she were riding an invisible pogo stick. "I can't wait, I can't wait, I can't wait!" she squealed. Not like a pig, just like her annoying self.

"What?" I said, confused.

"What's going on?" Haji came in behind me.

"Everyone, everyone! Come on. See!" Hammy motioned for everyone to gather around. "We found something amazing today." She held a bag close against her stomach.

"What is it?!" I shouted. I had observed that when people were hot and tired, they become impatient, me included. I would have to write that down in my notebook later.

"Peter, *this* is for you." Hammy pulled out material from a bag. It was faded but sturdy looking. She unfolded it. It was a field vest. Pockets, zippers, loops—it had *everything*. Attached to the field vest, small tools: brushes, a magnifying glass, a chisel and a hammer. It was like the vest was designed to hold those specific tools.

My eyes almost exploded out of my head. This wasn't just a field vest, it was a field vest for a *paleontologist.* It even looked like it had been worn by an actual paleontologist in the *field.*

"Try it on!" Hammy said. As she stood behind me, I lifted my arms and tucked them through the armholes.

"Oh my goodness! Oh my goodness! Oh my goodness! It's perfect!" L.B. screeched.

"Where did you find this?" Dad asked, amazed.

"I'm expert shopper!" Hammy replied, smiling. "Peter, you wear it when we go to museum in the summer. You will be very professional."

Notebook goes here!

"Hammy . . ." I couldn't get words out. I wanted to tell her how much I loved it. How perfect it was. Instead, I wrapped my long arms around her and held her tight.

When I had a chance later, I reached for my notebook and drew a sketch of the vest Hammy had bought me. I wrote: **BEST PRESENT EVER.**

Chapter 6

FREEDOM IN THE AIR

Ryan looked shocked when he got his "What I Hope to Become" writing assignment back. "What?" he exclaimed. "Only an A-! Mr. Costa, that is totally unfair. This is a solid A paper!"

Mr. Costa sighed wearily. His shirt today was completely wrinkled and he was wearing sweatpants. Surely this was a sign that he had finally given up. Mr. Costa came by my desk and handed me my paper.

An A. I smiled. It wasn't like I never got As, but this one felt particularly sweet.

Ryan grabbed my paper off my desk and looked at it. "Peter got an A?" he shouted. "There is no way his paper was better than mine! Did that stupid drawing of fossils get him an A? Additional artwork was not part of the criteria!"

Ryan threw my paper on the ground. My fossils were not stupid! *He* was stupid. Stephanie reached over and picked up my assignment.

"Outside, Ryan. Let's talk about this privately." Mr. Costa gestured for Ryan to step into the hallway.

Stephanie handed it back to me and said quietly, "Hey, that's a cool drawing."

I shook my head and put my hand up to indicate I was not in the mood. Why did Ryan always have to ruin everything?

"That's the last time I pay you a compliment," she said, turning her nose up.

Mr. Costa and Ryan left the classroom for the hallway, where they usually had their conversations. Mr. Costa still hadn't realized that the giant ventilation grille on the door gave them no privacy and that the class could hear every single word every time they went out there.

"Ryan, I don't appreciate you criticizing my marking. You can't compare your grade to Peter's grade. Everybody's grade is based upon the work that they did, given the criteria listed."

"Why isn't mine an A?" Ryan questioned.

"Yours was technically very sound," he said. "But it lacked personality and a certain *je ne sais quoi*. Do you know what I mean by *je ne sais quoi*?" Mr. Costa asked.

"Don't insult me, Mr. Costa. My last name's Gagnon."

"Ryan, it's not an insult, just a question."

"My mother is going to hear about this! She edited my paper, and she told me it was excellent!" Ryan spat out.

"Great! I'd love to hear about why your mother is doing your work for you," Mr. Costa said. "You know how I feel about students getting too much help from their parents."

A couple of students whispered, "Oooooh." Ryan had slipped up. I loved it.

"You are so unfair!" Ryan seethed as he stomped back into the class. Everybody was too scared to look directly at him.

I slipped my notebook out of my pocket. I wrote the date and a little scoreboard:

MR. COSTA 1, RYAN 0.

THURSDAY, JUNE 27, 10:10 A.M. (LAST DAY OF SCHOOL!)
CONDITIONS: GLORIOUS AND FREE

By the end of the week, Mr. Costa had finally given up and we were all practically tearing the room apart. On the last day of class, he wore flip-flops, shorts and a tank top. He was officially ready for the summer. Before recess, kids were sitting on top of desks, Liam went to the cloakroom to have a nap and Ryan was boasting about soccer.

"Coach put me up a level," he told Joe, who had foolishly been trapped into a soccer conversation with him. "I get to play in the Gold thirteen-year-old division next season."

"Congratulations," Joe replied sarcastically.

"Thanks," Ryan said smugly, missing the sarcasm completely. Joe looked at me and rolled his eyes.

To the few of us who still looked to him for direction, Mr. Costa said, "You may watch something on Netflix. Try to stick to the documentaries, though, okay?" We pulled up chairs, he turned his monitor and keyboard toward us, and I was positive he fell asleep with his eyes open.

Stephanie said, "Anybody know any good documentaries?"

"I do!" I piped up. "*When Dinosaurs Ruled like Kings!*"

"Seriously, Peter?" she asked, giving me her patented Stephanie look.

"It's good. I promise. I've seen it a dozen times and I'm not sick of it yet."

"Fine," she said. Everybody else shrugged their shoulders in agreement.

While we watched, I could tell that even Stephanie

thought that it was fascinating. It was a great way to spend the afternoon on the last school day of the year.

When the final bell rang, every child, teacher and administrator in Vancouver ran for the exit doors and didn't look back.

Hammy and Haji were waiting for us, in the usual spot.

L.B. ran up to them.

"Second grade in the books!" L.B. said. "Hopefully third grade will be *somewhat* more stimulating!"

I wanted to say, *I doubt it*. But I held my tongue.

L.B. tossed Haji her backpack. "One more time before summer holidays!" she said as she launched herself into a handspring off the Big Rock.

"Freedom Day, eh, Peter?" Haji said, smiling.

"Yup!" I said.

"What was the best part of fifth grade?" Haji asked.

"Today!"

"No, come on! Serious question."

"It's all in the past! I'm only thinking about the future now. I know the summer trip is going to be pretty awesome." I grinned.

"The trip is only a few days away," Hammy said as we started walking home. "We should start packing."

"Did you do any more research?" Haji asked.

"Oh, sure, I've read about all the attractions in Drumheller. There's a bunch of other stuff we could do besides the museum, but the museum is the most important thing, obviously."

"So many dinosaurs there, right, Peter?" Hammy said.

"So many dinosaurs!" I looked at the sky dreamily.

Chapter 7

ORGANIZATION—EXTREME

I finished up today's entry in my *Field Notes and Observations* journal and closed the book, feeling satisfied. I was done for the day, so I threaded the handle of my brush back through the elastic loop on the front of my vest and tucked my journal into my front left pocket. It was a perfect fit.

This particular journal contained two years' worth of notes. My style of note-taking had evolved over time. Get it? *Evolved?* That's an evolutionary science joke. First, the date. I mean, that goes without saying. Weather observations too. Then I made notes about what I saw or drew sketches of bone locations. I also numbered the bones in order of discovery.

My entries were now next level with the new excavation grid. The grid was kind of like a map to the excavation. I hadn't realized how much I needed it to make really accurate records. Real paleontologists use these grids all the time to draw out how they found bones, so that's what I did too. It helped keep things all in the right scale. I started off by using a ruler to draw out a grid in my notebook each time I excavated, but then I came to my senses, made one really good grid and photocopied it. Next I cut out the photocopied grids and glued them into my pages. Science is learning.

I also liked to label the bones with identifying markers while they were still in the sand—little pieces of cardboard I folded up into tents with the names of the bones written on them, along with their numbers. When I unearthed a bone, I placed a marker next to it. When I was all done and I was satisfied with my sketch, I would sit back and look at my work. I always felt like I had really accomplished something.

I couldn't wait to get to Drumheller and put all these skills to use. I tidied up my work area—the shovel, grid and bones were all returned to their usual spots—and lastly I covered the pit.

I dusted the sand off my hands, and Hammy opened the back door, holding the phone to her ear. I waved.

She motioned for me to come inside. "Your mom says

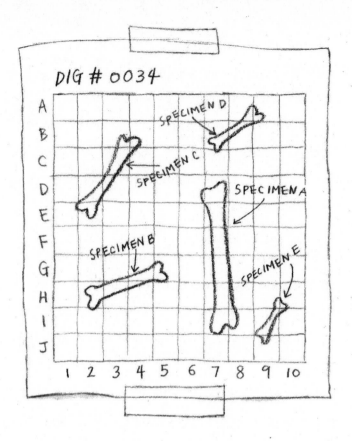

she dropped L.B. off at Dr. Stephanova's, so you come home now." When she said *Stephanova*, it sounded like *steppin' oba*.

I nodded. I gave both my pant pockets a tap.

"Hammy, I'm going to take the vest home because I need to pack it," I told her as I came inside.

"Good idea. You will need it!" She nodded. "We leave for Toronto in four days, right?"

"Toronto?" I said, surprised. "No, Drumheller!"

Hammy looked at me, confused. "I said, 'Drumheller.'"

"No . . . ah, never mind." I waved it off.

"You can walk home by yourself?" Hammy asked.

"Sure," I said. I took off the vest, draped it over my arm and walked home, daydreaming about the best way to chisel through ancient rock.

MONDAY, JULY 1, 2 P.M. (1 MORE DAY!)
CONDITIONS: CRYSTAL CLEAR BLUE SKY

"Peter!" Mom shouted at me. She was holding a duffel bag.

"What?" I was playing a game called *Dinosaur Extinction*, trying to solve puzzles while avoiding being eaten by a T. rex; it required great concentration and I hadn't even noticed she had come into my room.

"Why is your mouth all blue?"

I put down my tablet.

"Is it?" I thought for a minute before I realized why. "Oh, Joe and I had freezies." I probably should have told her that we had had them for lunch. But I didn't want her to ban me from going to his house all summer because together we made poor food choices.

She furrowed her brow.

"We're leaving bright and early tomorrow. It's time to start packing." She put the bag on my bed and turned to walk out of my room.

"Wait! You haven't packed yet?" I said, surprised. "You don't want *me* to pack, do you?"

"I think you are old enough to plan ahead, anticipate what you may need and then pack accordingly."

"What?" I had never packed for a trip before because we really didn't travel much. I suddenly missed the days when Mom would just do everything for me. If this was growing up, I was fine with staying young.

"If I were you, I'd definitely pack dinosaur underwear!" L.B. shouted from across the hall. She was playing an old Korean game called *yut* with Hammy in her room. You tossed four sticks in the air—one side was flat and one side was rounded. When the sticks landed on the ground, the number of flat sides facing up showed how many spaces you could move around the board.

"Mind your own business!" I yelled back. Hammy let out a yell and a clap. She must have landed in a good spot.

"Really, Peter, it's not that hard," Mom said. "Just think about what you need on a daily basis and pack it! We're gone about seven days, and I'll do laundry once."

"So four underwear sounds reasonable!" L.B. shouted, followed by a loud cheer. She could have just thrown her sticks gently, but instead she threw the sticks up in the air so high they always just missed the ceiling and came crashing down loudly. She thought it was funny, *every single time.*

I yelled back, "Be quiet! Stop throwing those sticks so high!"

"Where's the fun, then?" she cried back.

"No!" Hammy yelled, clearly disappointed.

"Got you, Hammy!"

Mom went across the hallway to close L.B.'s door. Their raucous game became somewhat muffled.

"I got you this." She handed me a black notebook with a large white coil along the side. It was much bigger than what I usually carried in my pocket. "I thought you might need a new one soon."

"Thanks, Mom." It was sturdy and the paper was thick. It felt nice in my hands. The coil was solid and could easily hold any pen or pencil.

"Also, I think for this trip, we're going to try to go old-school. No tablets on the drive." She gestured to my precious glowing screen. "Bring puzzles, books and games. Get packing," Mom said over her shoulder as she left me with my jaw hanging open.

The words washed over me again and again—*old-school,* *no tablet.* I felt like she had just scammed me. Butter me up with a fancy new notebook and then suddenly pull the rug out from under my feet.

It took a minute for it to sink in that I'd be forced to travel like a kid from the 1990s.

The idea was uncivilized and not cool at all, but I was determined not to let it ruin my holiday. After all, I *was* going to get to go on a real fossil dig—that was the important part in all of this.

What does any good scientist do when faced with a challenge? They read *books.* I looked at my bookshelf, which I affectionately called Dino Grotto. I thought it had a nice ring to it. I pulled *Fossil Dreams: A Young Scientist's Essential Guide* and *Paleontology for the Junior Enthusiast* off the shelf and packed them. I would be nothing without reference material. The bottom two shelves were crammed with books I had been collecting for years. On the other shelves, I had all my figurines lined up. The third shelf from the bottom had replicas of dinosaurs that lived during the Triassic period, 248 to 206 million years ago. Next shelf up, the Jurassic period, 200 to 146 million years ago. Finally, on top, the Cretaceous period, 146 to 65 million years ago. Within each shelf, I organized the figurines from left to right, largest in size to smallest—not the size of the figurines, but the size of the actual dinosaurs. To the untrained eye, it looked like random placement, but I knew better.

Something was wrong. The Allosaurus was on the Cretaceous shelf. It did *not* belong there. I knew who was responsible.

"L.B.!" I threw my door wide open and yelled across the hall. "Have you been messing with my dinosaurs?"

"Guilty as charged!" L.B. admitted, hollering back. "I thought the Allosaurus looked quite comfy next to the Iguanodon."

"How many times do I have to tell you? Leave Dino Grotto alone!"

"I'll try, but I am little and cannot control my impulses!"

I placed the Allosaurus back in its correct spot. Irritated, I returned to packing. My gear, I needed all of it. Vest, tools and especially my new notebook. Pens. Lots of pens. My duffel bag was almost full, but I still needed a few more things.

I carefully stepped to the door and peeked across the hallway to make sure L.B.'s door was still closed. Sticks clattered together, followed by L.B.'s distinctively annoying cheer. I gently closed my door. From my dresser, I quietly pulled out four of my best dinosaur underwear, folded them and packed them in my duffel bag too.

Chapter 8

(SCIENTIFIC) ADVENTURE AWAITS

TUESDAY, JULY 2, 8 A.M.

CONDITIONS: WARM, DRY AND A CHANCE OF
DINOSAUR SPOTTING

"Very beautiful day to start our trip!" Haji said happily as he slid the van door open.

Hammy winked at us and she plunked down her large handbag into the footwell of her seat in the middle row before she awkwardly got into the minivan.

"This will be quite an adventure!" L.B. chirped, smiling.

They had left a pile of suitcases and a large cooler by their front door. Dad struggled to stuff all of Hammy and Haji's suitcases into the back of the van among our suitcases, but, like a jigsaw puzzle, everything fit eventually and we headed out to the highway.

Around my seat in the back row I had a whole setup. A soccer ball at my feet, a few books to read, the Royal Tyrrell newsletter, a magnetic version of checkers, my Doodle-Board, a bottle of water, pencils and my crisp new journal. When we started driving, I flipped the pages around the coil and the paper gave off a crack noise, so I knew it was the first time the notebook had ever been opened. It felt like the start of something great. I wrote "Environmental Observations" across the cover page. This entire journal was going to be devoted to what I saw and what I learned on this trip. I didn't even pack my small coil notebook in my left pocket. It wouldn't be big enough to hold everything I was going to be seeing and doing.

On the highway, I started to observe my surroundings. I made some notes:

TREES. DOUGLAS FIR?

MOUNTAINS.

ROCKS. ASSORTED GRANITE.

TREES. HEMLOCK?

FARMS. CORN.

TREES. SPRUCE?

HAMMY IS SNORING.

HAJI IS ALSO SNORING.

MORE ROCKS.

I just stared out the window for a while. It didn't take me long to figure out that British Columbia is *huge* and a minivan can sometimes feel very small.

I tapped my pencil on the edge of the notebook, looking for new observations to make. Nothing. Finally, I got so bored I took a deep breath and decided I couldn't hold out any longer.

"Want to play hangman?" I asked L.B. cautiously. Talk about a new low. Asking L.B. to play with me. What I wouldn't have given for a tablet right now.

"Of course!" she replied happily, putting her book away.

I pulled out my DoodleBoard. I guess we could have used paper, but the DoodleBoard was the perfect thing for quick games. You could write on it with a special pen, or even a fingernail would work. When you were done, you just pressed a button to erase what you wrote.

"What's the topic?" I asked her.

"Different coding languages?" she suggested.

"I only know, like, two of those," I said.

She furrowed her brow. "Okay, South American lakes?"

"I don't know any!" I said, exasperated.

She turned her head and stared at me. "Petey, may I suggest *you* pick the topic?"

"Fine," I muttered. "Sports."

"Okay."

I drew out the hangman's gallows. Not a simple one, but a three-dimensional one. Since we had nothing but time, I also drew a rope.

L.B. smiled at it. "An unconventional approach to a classic game. I like it!"

"Whatever. Are you ready?"

"Petey, I have been waiting patiently for several minutes while you drew your very detailed hangman's gallows. Are you aware that it will be erased after this round?"

I gave her my best stink eye. Then I drew six perfectly spaced dashes.

L.B. looked at the screen for about four seconds.

"Soccer."

"You didn't even guess any letters! Don't you know how to play hangman?" I shouted.

"Am I right?"

"Yes! But that's not the point."

"*Aigoo*, why so loud, Peter?" Hammy said testily. I had woken her up. Since getting in the car, she had slept most of the way.

"Sorry, Hammy. L.B. doesn't know how to play hang-man."

"You need to choose words that aren't so obvious!" L.B. told me as she crossed her arms in disgust. "Try to *not* pick the sport you play at school *every day.*"

I dramatically clicked the board so that my gallows disappeared.

"Fine!" I thrust the DoodleBoard at her. "You have a turn!"

"Topic! Influential mathematicians!" she said loudly as she drew out four dashes, a slash to indicate a word break, and six more dashes. She set up her crudely drawn gallows with crooked, uneven lines and waited.

"Oh, I like that topic!" Dad smiled at us through the rearview mirror.

I didn't know any of those either. I ripped the board out of her hand and said, "I'm not playing anymore."

She frowned at me and then roughly pulled a dictionary from the seat pocket in front of her, opened it up and pretended to read.

I clicked to erase what she had written. I turned my body away from her so she couldn't see what I was doing. I drew another gallows. This time I drew a little girl with braids hanging from it. I'm not saying it was L.B., but it definitely *could* have been L.B. I smiled and clicked the board clean.

IN A VORTEX OF BOREDOM. TIME IRRELEVANT

When Hammy woke up, she started rummaging around her large purse, the kind a lot of Korean grandmothers carry.

"Let's listen to this." She pulled out a CD and handed it to my mom.

"What is it?" Mom asked.

"Korean audiobook," Hammy said.

"Korean audiobook sounds intriguing!" L.B. said.

I suppressed a groan. "You don't even speak Korean," I said quietly to L.B.

"It won't stop me from enjoying it," L.B. whispered back.

My mom put the CD in and said, "Maybe it's time we all learned a little Korean!"

"Good luck," Haji muttered.

Mom whipped around in her seat, like a mini tornado. "Why didn't you ever teach me Korean, Dad?" Her voice had a harshness to it, like burnt garlic.

"I tried," he said flatly. "More than once."

"Well, you didn't do a very good job!" she said. "I can't even order food in a Korean restaurant."

"That's because you were a terrible student," Haji said. Koreans have a way of being brutally blunt. Mom calls it the "Korean way." If you've put on weight, a Korean will tell you: *You look fat today*. If you have a new outfit and you're not sure about it, a Korean will tell you their opinion: *Those clothes look terrible on you*. The Korean way can be pretty rude.

"What?" Mom said, outraged.

"You were so stubborn! 'Why do I need Korean? We live in Canada!'" Haji said, mocking Mom's voice. "Ah, I gave up. Can't force somebody to do something they don't want to."

"A parent's job is to force their children to do things they don't want to do," Mom replied with seriousness. "That's the very definition of being a good parent."

I saw L.B. look up from her Rubik's Cube and stare at Mom.

I added a note to my *Environmental Observations.*

TRY TO CATCH L.B. PEELING STICKERS OFF HER RUBIK'S CUBE.

"Ah," Haji said, clicking his tongue. "You have your own Tiger Mama style. Not me." He looked out the window and flipped down the sunglass lenses attached to his regular glasses, as if he had flicked over a "closed" sign. He folded his arms tightly across his chest.

My eyes darted between Mom and Haji. You could feel indignation practically oozing out of every cell on Mom's body. Meanwhile, Haji smelled like triumph. There was a very awkward feeling in the car. The audiobook was playing in the background, but I don't think anybody was listening— it was just empty background noise.

"Did you know all polar bears are left-handed?" L.B. whispered as she tapped my arm. I looked over and saw that she had switched to reading *Four Thousand Amazing Facts to Share*—she took the "share" part a little too seriously.

When I didn't answer her, she soldiered on. "Somewhat related! Only 7 percent of human beings are left-handed."

"For goodness' sake, L.B. Leave me alone!" I replied impatiently.

She stiffened up and said, "Petey, as a young man of science, you should find these facts intriguing!"

"I *do* find them fascinating. Why don't you let me read them *by myself*?" I glared at her.

L.B. frowned at me and put her face deep into her book.

"When's the next rest stop?" Dad asked Mom.

"Not soon enough," Mom muttered.

"Ji Won," Hammy said loudly. Her eyes were closed, but she wasn't asleep.

I stared out the window.

"Ji Won," Hammy repeated.

Haji turned around and looked at me.

"Ji Won?" I asked, shrugging my shoulders.

Haji leaned as close as he could so he could whisper, "She's talking to you."

Hammy shook her head a bit, like she was shaking out loose cobwebs. "Ji Won. I mean, Peter . . ."

"Yes, Hammy?" I said, confused. Just like we never called L.B. by Charlotte, nobody ever called me by my

Korean name. Mom hadn't said anything, but she had turned around to watch and listen. Her eyebrows looked furrowed.

"I bought you something. It's a vest for you to wear on our trip." She had her eyes closed and I wasn't sure if she was awake or talking in her sleep.

I tilted my head and stopped to think. Did she mean the paleontology vest? The one she had already given me?

"Hammy, I—" I started to say, but Mom shook her head at me, as if she wanted me to stop. I closed my mouth and pursed my lips.

"Take nap," Haji said to Hammy as he patted her leg. She settled back into her seat.

That was weird. It ate away at me for a long time before I pulled out my journal. I wrote:

WHAT'S UP WITH HAMMY?

Chapter 9

CRAMPED VAN, SHORT TEMPERS

STILL TUESDAY, JULY 2. IS IT 4 P.M. OR 5 P.M.?
DOES IT MATTER?
CONDITIONS: UNBEARABLE HEAT

I opened the van door to a blast of heat. "Why's it so hot?" I complained. The sun was so bright I squinted and used my hands to shield my eyes from the light. We were stopping for the night in Peachland. We needed a break.

"This is as close to a desert climate as you will find in Canada," Mom chirped. "It's a microclimate!"

Just hearing the word *desert* made me pat my pocket for my inhaler.

"The human body needs plenty of vitamin D!" L.B. said. "Sunshine is the only natural source!"

"I'll go see if the room's ready," Dad said as he made his way to the hotel lobby.

Haji hopped out of the minivan, but Hammy looked shaky. I held Hammy's hand and helped her step down to the concrete. She let out a deep breath, reached into her purse, and pulled out her "Darth Visor"—the kind that shields her entire face from the sun—and slipped it onto her head. This look has caught on only with elderly Asian women. She sat down on a bench nearby. L.B. grabbed her skipping rope from the van and started jumping. Mom fanned herself with a magazine.

I scanned the surroundings. The hotel was called the Peachland Inn and Suites. It looked . . . old. They could have used it for a scene in a movie set in the 1950s. It was a two-level building and all the rooms faced the parking lot.

"Mom, please tell me that the rooms have air-conditioning," I begged.

"I sure hope so!" she said desperately.

Dad came back and started transferring suitcases from the trunk onto the worn, faded carpet of the luggage cart. I knew I should have been helping, but I was too busy melting into a human puddle of sweat on the sidewalk.

L.B. stopped jumping rope and proclaimed, "I'll help!" But all she did was hop onto the corner of the luggage rack, hold on to a bar and wait for somebody to push her.

"Peter?" Dad asked hopefully, wiping his brow. The back of his shirt was soaked and his glasses were steamed up.

I slowly moved my sticky body and grabbed the edge of the cart.

"The elevator is way down at the end of the building," Dad told me.

L.B. turned to look at me impatiently.

As I put my hands on the cool brass frame of the cart, I suddenly had the feeling that it was time for a little experiment. Everybody knows that momentum is generated by mass and velocity. After doing some quick calculations of the total weight of the suitcases on the cart, I decided that L.B.'s additional weight was so slight it would have no effect on the momentum I could generate. If this ride was going to be awesome, I had to jump on the edge of the cart, adding extra mass, to really get this thing flying.

"L.B., how many seconds do you think it will take us to reach the end of the building?" My hands held the frame tightly and my shoes dug into the cement.

"Five seconds." She grinned mischievously.

"Okay, I'll try for four." I inhaled deeply, getting in as much oxygen as I could for the sprint and pushed as hard as I could to start the wheels rolling as quickly and efficiently as possible.

"Faster!" yelled L.B. as she leaned to the side, trying to catch the breeze.

I was trying to run as fast as Dromiceiomimus, which, considering its resemblance to the modern emu, meant my legs were flying.

"Careful!" Mom yelled.

I slowed down the cart by jumping off, halting all the hard-earned momentum I had generated.

"Slow is not fun." L.B. hopped off too.

"We made it in six seconds anyway." I shrugged, happy with my pace. "Even when I killed the speed."

She helped me push the cart the rest of the way to our room.

When we opened the door, my eyes darted around the room. It was a very big space, and it had three beds lined up against one wall. The bed linens looked old and faded, and the room smelled musty. Traveling didn't seem as glamorous in real life as it did on TV. But under the window, there was an air conditioner blasting frigid air, so it suddenly became the best hotel room in the world. Nobody was going to move me away from the air conditioner until I was as close to hypothermia as I could tolerate.

Mom and Dad transferred bags from the luggage cart into our room and everybody found a place to sit down. Except me. I was still standing so I could lift the back of my shirt and let the cool air waft up my spine.

"I'm somewhat peckish," L.B. said as she moved her bag near the window.

"Hammy make you something." She opened up one of her suitcases. It was completely packed with food. There were maybe two dozen packages of instant Korean noodles. "Pick one," she said to L.B.

I saw my favorite brand of black bean noodles. "Can I have one too?"

"Of course!" Hammy said. She seemed to have perked up.

"How are you going to cook these?" Mom asked.

"Just boil water!" Hammy said. She pulled an electric kettle out of her suitcase. "All these noodles have own bowl already."

"I'll do it!" Mom said quickly as she tried to take the kettle from Hammy.

"I can do!" Hammy said testily as she shouldered Mom out of the way and filled the kettle with water.

L.B. handed Hammy a packet and said, "*Ahnmepgae haejuseyo.*"

We all stopped and looked at her. Haji roared with laughter and Hammy looked astounded.

"What did she just say?" I asked Haji.

"She just said to not make hers too spicy!" Haji told me, unable to suppress his joy. "L.B., when did you learn to say that?" He kept shaking his head, as if he couldn't believe what he had just heard.

"From listening to the Korean audiobook," L.B. said simply.

"L.B. so smart!" Hammy said warmly as she patted the top of L.B.'s head.

I gritted my teeth, which had started to chatter. I had had enough of the air conditioner anyway. I walked up to my bag and pulled out my journal. I flopped down on the floor and wrote:

ROAD TRIPS SOUND FUN, BUT THEY ARE NOT.

PEACHLAND IS HOT AND EXTREMELY UNCOM-FORTABLE. IT SHOULD BE CALLED BAKELAND.

L.B. LEARNED KOREAN IN FIVE HOURS. BRAT.

HOTEL ROOMS ARE DEPRESSING.

I slammed my book shut and waited impatiently for my noodles.

My skin was sticky *everywhere*, and I was tired from our day of traveling. We went out for a real dinner after our quick snack of instant noodles and then wandered around downtown Peachland, which, thankfully, was just one short strip of shops. After that, nobody was in the mood to do anything except go to sleep. I got my pajamas out of my suitcase and lined up for my turn in the washroom.

Even L.B. was too tired to make any obnoxious remarks. She sat quietly on the bed, holding her toothbrush. Haji was taking forever. He was really brushing hard and loud and making all these noises. You learn a lot about a person when you share a hotel washroom with them. The things I was learning I really, really didn't need to know. He did this thing with his throat that I think of as Korean-style phlegm management and I cringed.

"Are you sure you're going to sleep on the floor, Peter?" Mom asked me for the fifth time. She was climbing in to her bed.

"Yes!" I puffed up the flat hotel pillow.

"There's room in L.B.'s bed."

L.B. smiled coyly and patted the empty spot next to her.

"Nope! I'm fine!"

L.B. frowned.

"Okay, then, if you're comfortable," Mom agreed reluctantly as she turned off the lights. "Good night, everybody."

We all muttered our various forms of good night. Hammy and Haji had fallen asleep before the room went dark.

I adjusted my blanket and settled in. Even though I was sleeping on the world's thinnest and dirtiest carpet, I fell asleep instantly.

When I woke up, the light from a bedside lamp was shining on me and I heard whispered voices. My eyes were sticky but I pried one open to sneak a peek at the alarm clock; it was 4:05 a.m.

All the adults were surrounding Hammy, but L.B. was still asleep in her bed, curled up into a tight ball. Hammy was dabbing her nose with a tissue. I was very groggy and couldn't tell what was happening for a few seconds.

"Please don't wake the kids!" Mom said desperately.

"Let's all relax . . . go back to sleep," Haji said gently, encouraging Hammy to lie back down.

"No!" Hammy hissed, clutching her tissue.

"Mom, what's wrong?" my mom asked.

"I . . . I don't know," Hammy whispered. "I opened my eyes. I didn't remember this room. I got so scared."

"It's okay, Mom. We're in Peachland. We're traveling to Drumheller."

"Peter and museum. Dinosaurs." Hammy nodded as if she finally understood.

"Yes, Peter and the museum."

"Okay, I remember," Hammy said. She looked like she was going to settle back down under the blanket.

"Let's try to get a bit more sleep. We've got to get on the road soon," Dad whispered.

"I'm glad the kids didn't wake up," Mom said as she got back into bed.

I stayed as still as possible and tried so hard to keep my breathing regular and calm. Mom was wrong. I was awake, and I had seen and heard everything.

Chapter 10

DEFINE *HOLIDAY*

Dad shook me awake and waved a paper bag in front of my face.

"Breakfast!"

I threw my blanket over my head. "What time is it?"

"Five forty-five."

"Five forty-five!" I yelled.

"We have a lot of ground to cover today. We need to get an early start." Dad gave my shoulder a little poke.

The paper bag crinkled.

"I asked for extra bacon in yours." The heavenly smell was impossible to ignore.

I flicked the blanket off my face. "You're not playing fair." Name one person who won't get up for extra bacon. I felt like every muscle in my body was rebelling against the act of sitting up, but I was a slave to the power of the bacon.

I rubbed my eyes and looked around the room. Everybody was already up. L.B. waved and pointed to her mouth, full of bagel and peanut butter, as if to explain why she wasn't talking, and all the adults sipped coffee. Mom flipped through a newspaper.

With some effort, I unwrapped the paper around my sandwich and took a big bite, closing my eyes as I chewed. My brain was not working. I must have gone back to sleep after all the fuss earlier this morning and I wondered if anybody else had managed to go back to sleep. Nobody was talking and Dad seemed to have ordered himself an extra-large coffee, so I guessed he had just stayed awake.

Hammy was dressed and took a small bite from her muffin.

"Everything okay, Hammy?" I asked.

"Oh, sure, Peter. Everything's fine." She smiled, but I could see the tired look in her eyes.

As I popped the last bit of sandwich into my mouth, Dad pulled some math books out of the side pocket of his suitcase and said, "Here, just do a few pages."

I felt my jaw fall open, and a piece of bacon dropped out of the corner of my mouth. I was so shocked I didn't even retrieve it off the floor.

"I thought we were in a rush!"

"There's always time for math." Dad placed a book in front of me.

Just as I was going to protest, Mom said, "Summer learning loss is a real thing."

School had ended exactly six days ago. How could I have possibly forgotten anything? Scowling, I picked up the book.

"Pencil," I said through gritted teeth as I held out my hand. Dad reached into his suitcase and dropped one into my palm.

"You too, L.B.," Dad said as he handed her a workbook.

Peanut butter was crusted on her lip and she looked surprised, as if she thought she was excused from this sort of thing, and I smiled. It was only fair. If I had to suffer, so did she.

She snatched the book out of Dad's hands. She stomped to the corner of the room with her half-eaten bagel hanging out of her mouth and irritably flopped down on the floor. Treating the book very roughly, she slammed the spine down on the ground and pushed along the length of its pages with the palm of her hand so it would stay open.

"L.B. . . . ," Mom said reproachfully as she zipped up a suitcase. "Your math tutor suggested this series of books for you while we were on holidays. It must be good."

L.B. ignored her and focused on scribbling furiously in her book. When Mom turned her back, she quietly muttered, "Some holiday." It wasn't loud enough for our parents to hear, but I heard it.

The lead of my pencil broke and I looked up at the ceiling in exasperation. By the time I found another pencil, L.B. had closed her book shut and said, "Done!" She left the book on the floor and went to go sit next to Hammy.

I hadn't even finished two questions yet!

"You want to play?" L.B. asked Hammy as she stuck her hands out, palms up. She was asking Hammy to play their hand-slapping game. They thought it was fun, but I thought it looked pretty much like hitting somebody for no reason. People go to jail for that.

Before Hammy could answer, Dad handed L.B. a book called *Engineering: A Very Long History* and said, "Let Hammy rest. It's going to be a long drive in the van today. Read this while we wait for Peter—he might take some time."

I quietly fumed.

"We play later, okay?" Hammy said, patting L.B.'s arm. She closed her eyes and leaned against her pillow.

While I was concentrating on finishing the stupid math questions, the rest of the family discussed our next stop. I just heard some talk about Banff and hot springs but didn't ask any questions because I knew everybody was waiting for me.

After I finished my required two pages, I closed the book and tossed it on the floor on top of L.B.'s book.

Dad glared at me, picked up our books and carefully put them back in the suitcase. "You'll thank me one day."

I turned my back and was about to roll my eyes when I caught sight of Hammy. She looked really out of it. Since she had finished her muffin, she'd just been sitting on the bed, propped against a pillow. L.B. was now curled up with her head on Hammy's lap. I couldn't quite place my finger on what was wrong. Maybe she was just tired from that weird wake-up last night, but then again, what was that wake-up all about anyway? The scientist in me couldn't help but realize that I needed to collect more data by keeping a detailed record of facts and observations. This was the only way to come to an accurate conclusion.

I wanted to get all this information down in my journal while my thoughts were still fresh. I discreetly held my notebook by my side and headed to the washroom.

"Why are you taking your journal to the bathroom?" L.B. asked. "Do you need *reading material?*" She snickered. I was beyond annoyed. I had important data to record! Why couldn't she just keep her big mouth shut for once?

"None of your business!" I said testily. I had been hoping for some privacy. But in a hotel room with six people, privacy is about as rare as finding a complete fossil of an ankylosaur.

"Don't be too long, Peter," Mom said, rummaging through her purse. "We're leaving soon. It's well past six o'clock now. You need to get dressed and we really need to get on the road."

"I'll take as long as I need!" I declared.

"Turn on the fan!" L.B. giggled.

I stomped into the bathroom, turned on the fan just to humor my annoying sister and sat down on the toilet. I was doing my business, but not the kind everybody else thought I was doing. I opened my notebook and started writing:

HAMMY DEMONSTRATING UNUSUAL BEHAVIOR.

FORGETTING THINGS, GENERALLY TIRED.

SLEEPING ALL THE TIME.

CALLED ME JI WON? WHAT THE HECK?

4 A.M. CRYING EPISODE.

WATCH MORE.

6:30 A.M.

Once we were back in the car, we drove out of the Okanagan Valley and headed north toward the Rocky Mountains. As we drove, we passed orchards where I could see peaches hanging from tree branches, and vineyards where rows and rows of grapevines were planted in tidy straight lines. The highway followed the edge of a lake, and I watched boats and Jet Skiers flying along the surface of the water.

Once in a while Mom would point and say, "Wow, look at this scenery!"

"So beautiful!" Haji agreed.

Hammy even seemed to perk up a little; I could tell she was taking it all in as she stared out the window.

The Korean audiobook droned on in the background while I kept myself busy reading my favorite paleontology books.

"It's the Rocky Mountains!" Mom said excitedly, pointing out the window when the landscape seemed to suddenly change from gray rocky formations to a deep penetrating blue.

I looked up from my book and shrugged.

"Big deal," I said. I just *needed* to get to Drumheller and nothing else mattered.

"You don't think it's beautiful?" Mom asked incredulously.

"Kinda just looks like Vancouver," I said.

L.B. peered out the window and said, "I disagree, Petey. These mountains are clearly more majestic than the local

North Shore Mountains. The average elevation of the local mountains near Vancouver is merely about 1,700 meters, or 5,500 feet. The average elevation of the Rocky Mountains is 4,400 meters, or 14,400 feet. More than double." She paused and looked up to the sky. "That's 2.59 times as large, to be exact, using the rounded metric numbers. So, clearly, not the same at all."

Mom turned to L.B. and smiled approvingly.

I hated her big mouth and I hated her big brain.

"Shut up," was all I could manage as a comeback. I pulled out my Royal Tyrrell newsletter and read it for the fifty-ninth time.

Chapter 11

STEAMY, LIKE THE MESOZOIC ERA

Things changed when I saw the "Welcome to Alberta" sign. I glanced at the clock; we had been on the road for almost six hours, stopping only for pee breaks and drive-thrus. Nervous excitement flooded my stomach and it felt like it was doing a gymnastics floor routine now that we were finally in the same province as the Royal Tyrrell Museum.

Right after crossing the provincial border, we came to the famous mountain town of Banff. The most notable thing about it was that it was full of tourists. Absolutely jam-packed. The streets were lined with giant luxury tour buses. Everywhere I looked, people meandered with cameras strapped around their necks and maps in their hands. We didn't stop in town, which was probably okay because, looking around, it didn't even seem like we could have found a parking spot if we wanted one. Instead, we kept driving until we were on a narrow road on the side of a very steep cliff.

Dad stopped the van in front of a building called the Banff Upper Hot Springs. I didn't understand what was happening. I just followed like a Stegosaurus with its walnut-sized brain as we all got out of the car, stretched our backs and legs, and headed for the front doors.

The glass doors slid open and we were greeted by a strange smell. The air seemed unusually thick and hazy.

"We need six rental suits," Mom told the woman at the front desk.

I froze. Rental suits? What was she talking about?

After sizing everybody up, the woman stepped into a back room and reemerged with her arms loaded. She handed each of us a bathing suit. Not just any bathing suit, but a bathing suit previously worn by *somebody else*. Worse still, it was a retro-looking one-piece, and everybody's looked identical— navy blue with a white stripe across the thighs. Imagine the six of us all wearing the same thing. I was wearing the same suit as my sister! As my *mother*! As my *grandmother*!

Hello, humiliation. My name is Peter Lee and I'm about to wear the same bathing suit as all the girls in my family. I held the suit limply in my hand and felt deflated, like a shriveled balloon, as I followed Dad and Haji into the men's changeroom. As soon as Haji started to undress, I turned my back to look away. I'm close to him, but not *that* close.

Still, I said nothing. Too stunned by what was happening to me to form even the most basic words.

"We look so cute!" Mom shrieked as we emerged from the changerooms one by one. "We have to take a picture."

There we all were, standing in front of a steaming pool of boiling-hot, funky-smelling water while a stranger took a picture of us on my mom's cell phone. Worse still, we lined up according to height. My mother was the queen of embarrassing, awkwardly staged family photos.

"Everybody say 'fossils'!" Mom instructed. *Click.*

We headed to the pools as I scanned my surroundings suspiciously. "What's the big deal with the hot springs?" I finally asked.

"The water is heated by a natural geothermal source," L.B. said. "Some believe the waters contain healing properties. I'm not sure about *that*, but it can be quite relaxing to soak in warm water."

"Oh," I answered. So we're here to have a bath with strangers. Gross. I wished I had been listening more closely—and not doing math—when they were discussing it. I would have objected.

I stood back and watched Hammy and Haji settle into the water. They didn't seem bothered by the scalding temperatures or the fact that you were basically forced to sit shoulder to shoulder with random strangers because it was so busy.

"Ah." Hammy sighed. It was the happiest she had looked in the last two days. "So good."

"*Cha!*" Haji said. "Very nice!"

"Petey! Let's go to the children's area!" L.B. said as she grabbed my hand.

"Stay together!" Dad yelled as he tentatively stepped into the water.

I reluctantly followed L.B. I was a bit too old and a bit too tall for the children's area, but the woman at the front desk said the temperature there was a few degrees cooler, and it was much less busy than the adult side. I cautiously dipped my toes in the water. It was still boiling hot! Liar!

"L.B.! Careful, it's so hot!" I told her.

L.B. stomped her foot in the water and said, "Petey, it's a *hot* spring." Then she threw her whole body into the pool, making a giant *splat* in the water. She disappeared underwater for a second before she resurfaced, laughing.

I sat on the edge of the pool and worked my toes, then my feet and then my calves into the water. This whole trip

I'd been hot. The last thing I wanted to do was sit in a giant tub of hot water with a hundred strangers of unknown hygiene. This sounded like a public health emergency waiting to happen.

Miserably, I watched L.B. do forward somersaults, backward somersaults and handstands in the water. She did torpedo swims across the whole length of the children's area, back and forth like a dolphin, weaving her way around other kids. She finally noticed I hadn't gotten into the water and swam up to me.

"What's wrong, Petey?" L.B. asked.

"This stinks."

"The water does contain sulfuric elements—"

I cut her off. "No, no! Well, yes, the water smells funny, but I meant, this *sucks*. Why are we wasting our time here?"

"Come in the water, Petey. It's fun!"

"How is hot water fun?"

"The heat is relaxing," she replied. "You have to try it to believe it. I am now a believer!"

Funny, she didn't look *relaxed* at all; she hadn't stopped moving since she first plunged herself in the water.

"L.B., I don't want to relax. I want to see dinosaurs!" I cried. "We're so close. Why can't we just get there already!"

"Petey, we'll get there soon." She tried to reassure me. "But while we're here, we should enjoy the moment."

She paused and looked at me sulking.

"Will you give me a piggyback, *please?*" she asked with her best cute face and least-annoying voice. "I asked very nicely and didn't jump on you without warning."

I felt myself crumbling. "Okay, fine."

She pulled me into the pool and then leaped on my back, shrieking into my ear as we both tumbled into the water.

3 P.M.

CONDITIONS: BUOYANT AND REFRESHED (TELL NO ONE!)

After returning our wet bathing suits, everybody felt rejuvenated. Haji and Hammy had a dewy glow to their complexions and it seemed like Haji had a little extra bounce in his step. Hammy seemed *okay*, but my keen eye was still on her. *I* was actually feeling pretty good too. The warm, moist air was really great for me, and my lungs felt all relaxed and so calm. The forty-five minutes in the boiling pools was just what we all needed. We were ready for the last push to Drumheller.

There was good energy in the van when we got back on the road. We were all kind of light-headed and giddy, and I'm sure we'd all absorbed some brain-altering chemicals from the water. As we drove away from the hot springs, Mom scrolled through the pictures from today.

"Look at this! This is a great photo!" Mom turned around and showed us the picture of the six of us lined up according to height. I was blinking. Big surprise. L.B. looked absolutely adorable with her hair in a high, stylish braid, a perfect smile and one hand on her hip. Revolting.

After driving for another two hours, we descended the mountain range and the landscape changed. I sat up in my seat. Things looked different here. I felt it instantly.

Gone were the huge mountains with snowcapped peaks, gone were the forests of trees. The landscape became an eerie kind of brown, gray and muted green, all blended together. The rolling hills off the highway were layered sedimentary rock; they reminded me of those Jell-O cubes that somebody always brings to a party, but much less colorful. It was amazing. Finally, this was some scenery to get excited about.

We were in the Alberta Badlands; I knew it. Out there in those weird hills, I was going to get to hunt for real fossils. They would name the new discovery "Peterolocyphis" or "Petersauralophus" or something awesomely cool like that. I would become famous and a camera crew would follow me around as I worked and talked about my incredible finds.

I suddenly remembered that I should be taking notes. I fished my journal out of my bag and wrote:

LEAVING ROCKY MOUNTAINS.

HOT SPRINGS ARE NOT TOO TERRIBLE.

APPROACHING ALBERTA BADLANDS. YES!

DRASTIC CHANGE IN LANDSCAPE. LAYERED SEDIMENTARY ROCK. SO COOL.

ARID CONDITIONS.

LITTLE TO NO VEGETATION.

The rocks had me mesmerized. On the side of the road, I saw the "Welcome to Drumheller" sign with a giant T. rex picture on it. I felt giddy. I couldn't help myself. An entire town devoted to dinosaur enthusiasts. I'd spent years dreaming about it, and we were finally here!

"These rocks are quite interesting, aren't they?" L.B. piped up. "The layering of sediment—"

"Sh!" I hissed and cut her off. She was ruining my moment.

"Peter, she's allowed to talk," Mom scolded.

"Can't I just enjoy the scenery with some peace and quiet?" I asked.

"Oh, *now* you find the scenery interesting . . . ," Mom muttered.

As we continued the last part of our drive into town, I eagerly looked around at everything Drumheller had to offer, and I knew this was going to be my kind of place. We were finally here. And tomorrow I'd get to experience, first-hand, being a paleontologist.

Chapter 12

DREAMS DO COME TRUE

I had a lousy night's sleep. We'd arrived too late for us to do any sightseeing last night, so we just ate dinner at the restaurant off the hotel lobby. I was really disappointed that we couldn't leave our hotel—I mean, I wasn't *crying* but I was upset—so Dad said I could order anything I liked for dinner. I decided to see just how good the beef in Alberta really was, and I ordered prime rib. Dad just about choked when I asked for an extra Yorkshire pudding.

My parents had rented a giant family suite with two bedrooms and two sofa beds in the living room. The sofa bed was possibly worse than sleeping on the floor in Peachland. It had felt like trying to sleep on the armored back of an Euoplocephalus. I counted fourteen unique and distinctive lumps all working together to make my sleep uncomfortable.

The thing about Alberta is, the air is dry, and the air in the hotel room is even drier with the air-conditioning running all the time. I had felt so bad in the night that I even had to creep out of bed, find my inhaler and take a puff. At least L.B. and I didn't have to share a bed.

"Good morning, Petey!" L.B. turned on her side, lifted her head and gave me a big, goofy grin.

"Stop being so perky," I moaned.

"Already arguing," Mom grumbled. She was addressing her urgent need for coffee and struggling to separate the paper filters.

L.B. hopped down from the creaky sofa bed and threw open the curtains.

"What a glorious day!" she proclaimed with her hands on her hips.

"How can you be so chipper in the mornings?" I squinted and rubbed my eyes.

"We're on a wonderful adventure with beloved family. Seeing new things and free from our usual routine."

"Your big day is finally here, Peter. The museum will be a wonderful learning experience for everybody! Shouldn't you be more excited?" Mom asked.

I sat up on the lumpy sofa bed and threw off my blanket. How could I have forgotten? I shook the cobwebs out of my head and sprang out of bed. I grabbed my favorite dinosaur T-shirt and put it on. I was already wearing my dinosaur underwear. It may have been too much on most other days, but today, I also put on my dinosaur socks.

Lastly, I looked for my field vest. I had made sure to pack it carefully so that none of my tools came loose during the trip. Gingerly, I lifted it out of my duffel bag and slipped it on.

Standing in front of the full-length mirror in the hotel room, waiting for everybody else to get ready, I beamed at my reflection. I was so ready for this. I saw my hat sitting on the arm of the sofa and stuffed it in my backpack too. That would have been dumb to forget the hat!

"There's a free continental breakfast in the lobby," Mom said, staring at a flyer on the desk.

"I'm not hungry." Me, not interested in food. I could hardly believe it. My impatience to get to the museum was real.

"Well, *I'm* hungry, so let's go get some food. You know how much I love free breakfast!" Dad said. It was true. He went to Denny's by himself on his birthday to get a free meal. The man had no shame.

"We're going to need some energy if we're going to explore the museum this morning before your afternoon dig, right?" Mom reminded me.

"Fine," I muttered. "Let's go get our free food." I tapped my foot anxiously and waited for my family to get organized.

9:30 A.M.
ROYAL TYRRELL MUSEUM (ENOUGH SAID!)

My face was practically glued to the window on the drive from the hotel to the museum. I didn't even care that the sun was oppressively hot and the air was the driest and dustiest I had ever experienced in my whole life. I scrawled into my journal:

ACTUAL FIELDWORK DAY! YES!

EXCITEMENT LEVEL: EXTREME.

BEST DAY EVER.

As soon as Dad parked, I leaped out of the van and sprinted through the parking lot. The museum was nestled among the distinctive hills of the Alberta Badlands, right at the top edge of a steep cliff that was part of a natural crescent formation of rocks. The museum itself was an immense structure, square and angular. The dark glass panels covering the front facade reflected the sun's bright rays. The modern and the ancient, all right here. A huge statue of a Pachyrhinosaurus greeted me outside the

112

building's entrance. I would have hugged it if I could have. Instead, I patted its side respectfully and solemnly. I felt like yelling "Hurry up!" so many times as my family lagged behind, but Hammy and Haji really couldn't go any faster.

L.B. ran up to the statue and climbed it. She wrapped her legs around the neck of the poor Pachyrhinosaurus and yelled, "Look at me!" The sequins on her smiley-faced-emoji T-shirt reflected the sunlight.

"Wow, scary statue!" Haji said, pointing. He looked at me and smiled.

"The thing on top is even scarier," I mumbled.

"Let's take a family picture!" Mom said.

"Seriously?" I shouted. "Now?"

"If not now, when?" She was completely oblivious to my desperate need to get inside immediately. She pulled out a selfie stick from her bag.

I prayed she wouldn't line us up by height.

"Stand in front of the Royal Tyrrell sign, Peter." She waved her hand at me and motioned me over. "L.B., get down!"

"Mom!" I complained.

"You will want this photo memory later, I am sure," L.B. said to me as she swung herself off the Pachyrhinosaurus.

"One picture!" I shouted. "Just one!"

We shuffled into position while my mom pointed the stick high in the air.

"Everybody say 'T. rex!'" Mom said as she snapped the photo. I tried hard not to roll my eyes or blink.

"Tickets! Now!" I said urgently and pushed everybody toward the building.

The girl at the ticket booth greeted us with an enthusiastic, *"Ni hoa ma!"* Everybody in my family slouched and glared at her with either a blank stare or an evil eye. She switched gears, lifted up her laminated piece of paper that said "Greetings in 100 Different Languages," looked the paper over and started to say, *"Konnich—"*

Mom held up her hand and said flatly, "We speak English."

The girl looked embarrassed. "Oh, sorry."

When we finally walked into the museum, I was greeted by the powerful stance of an Albertosaurus with its ferocious jaws open. It took me a moment to gather myself and to finally appreciate that we were here. Dinosaur heaven in Canada. Before me, a cavernous museum filled with all things dinosaur. Life couldn't get much better. I knew most of my classmates didn't like dinosaurs anymore, or at least that's what they said, but I had been in love from the moment I could say "Jurassic," and the love had never died. I didn't care who knew it.

Because I was in the afternoon session of the Junior Scientist Dig, we had the whole morning to explore the museum. I could still hardly believe that I was going to go and dig for dinosaur fossils! An actual dig for real bones. It was true fieldwork. The thing I was most excited about was the prospect of using a hammer and chisel on ancient rock. Imagine how exhilarating it must be to be chipping away and then suddenly start to expose the distinctive edges of a fossil that had been hidden and obscured for millions of years. Soon I wouldn't have to imagine it anymore, because I was going to do it.

My excavation pit at home was just a very small warm-up for the real thing. I had been preparing and studying for this day for ages, maybe even my whole life. I was so excited; my intestines were quivering with anticipation. Or maybe that was the free hotel breakfast coming back to say hi.

The collection was beyond all my wildest dreams. I spent the morning gawking at the immense scale of the fossils. When I saw the T. rex fossil they call "Black Beauty," emotions overwhelmed me. I touched the corner of my eye and, I swear, it was almost wet. It was the most beautiful thing I had ever seen. The body encased in rock, frozen in time. I loved the way the bones curved into an arc. So elegant, even in death.

"Look at this one," Dad said, reading the information next to the fossil of a large sauropod. "Hey, Peter, did you know that the Brontosaurus might actually be an Apatosaurus? Scientists are not sure if the early specimen they found and named Brontosaurus, like, over a hundred years ago, was classified correctly. *But* new research may suggest that the Brontosaurus did, in fact, exist?"

"Yes, Dad, *everybody* knows that."

"Well, sorry, I'm not as well-read on the subject as you. Did you know that, L.B.?" He looked miffed.

She glared up at him. "Obviously. It is one of the most well-known controversies in paleontology."

Dad didn't read any more information signs to us.

We slowly made our way through the displays. Each section had so many different vignettes, each telling its own story, and I wanted to read everything.

"Come on, Hammy," L.B. urged. Hammy had been sitting on a bench while we were in the terrestrial Paleozoic zone. It's like she didn't even care about the Dimetrodon. Probably because it wasn't *technically* a dinosaur. It was a reptilelike mammal that predated the real dinosaurs. She went to grab Hammy's hand.

"Okay, L.B., Hammy just needs to rest." She smiled wearily.

It reminded me that I was pretty tired too. I glanced up at the clock and realized we had been wandering around the museum for hours.

"I think now would be a good time for lunch," Dad said.

Who needed lunch? My eyes were feasting on dinosaur fossils, but I followed my family to the cafeteria anyway.

12:10 P.M.

I didn't think I was hungry, but when I saw it on the menu, I had to have the Jurassic Snack Pack, which came in a paper box decorated with a dinosaur scene. Oh, sure, it was just a cheeseburger, apple slices and a small juice box, but I did get a free sticker. I didn't realize how exhausted I was until I sat down to eat. The snack pack was just what I needed to give me the energy for the rest of the afternoon.

"It's almost time—come on!" I stood up.

"Peter, we still have twenty minutes," Mom said through a mouthful of salad.

"I want to be first in line!" I waved the sheet of paper around with the instructions for dig participants. "Chop-chop!" I clapped my hands and ran around and cleaned up everybody's lunch trays, even if they weren't exactly done.

The instructions outlined that we were to stand next to a classroom door marked "Laboratory 1A" a few minutes before one o'clock, and without even looking at a map, I just *knew* where to go. Not a soul was there.

"Yes." I did a small fist pump. "First in line." I was obviously the most excited kid in the whole group.

While waiting for the door to open, I started to have that antsy feeling in my legs, like I couldn't stand still.

Other kids started to gather the closer it got to one o'clock. I counted eleven others, all prepared with small backpacks and looking *almost* as excited as me. There was even one boy who spoke with an English accent! I nodded to him out of sheer respect. An international dinosaur enthusiast—he must have been hard-core. I noted proudly to myself that *nobody* else had professional gear like I did. The English boy gazed at my vest longingly.

When the door to Laboratory 1A finally opened, I thought I heard music from the angels and I saw a heavenly bright light. The woman who opened the door was wearing just what I imagined she should be wearing. A wide-brimmed hat, *check*. A khaki-colored shirt with lots of pockets, *check*. Cargo pants that matched, *check*. Hiking boots, *check*. Clipboard in hand, *check*. She looked perfect. Scientific and professional in a casual, outdoorsy kind of way that let you know she did fieldwork.

I barely said goodbye to my family and nodded vaguely when Mom said, "Meet you back here at four!" They fell away from my consciousness. I could think of nothing but dinosaurs, fossils, layered sedimentary rock, trowels and chisels. I had just walked into a scientific laboratory with a huge fossil encased in rock lying on a worktable. I sighed with satisfaction. This was everything I had been waiting for.

Chapter 13

FIELDWORK IS NOT FOR WUSSIES

1 P.M.

CONDITIONS: STILL HOT . . . HOW DO PEOPLE
LIVE LIKE THIS?

"Who's excited?" the well-dressed paleontologist asked.

The twelve of us shouted, "Me!"

"Hello, everyone. I'm Kendra. I'll be your dig leader today."

I wondered if this was the same Kendra who was to receive all the contest submissions.

"Are you a real paleontologist?" the boy with the English accent asked her.

She smiled. "Yes. Yes, I am. This is my third year working at the Royal Tyrrell Mu—"

"What dinosaurs have you discovered?" some rude child interrupted.

"Well, I haven't *discovered* a new species or anything, but I have been involved in quite a few large excav—"

"So, you've personally never found a fossil?" a girl asked.

"No . . . I—" she started.

"Hey!" I yelled. "Let her talk!"

I got a couple of suspicious looks from the other kids, but Kendra looked relieved and said, "Thank you. Great vest, by the way." She winked at me and my face flushed. "Let's begin, shall we?"

All of the kids eventually settled down and finally Kendra could talk without being constantly interrupted.

"I thought we'd start our afternoon in this lab," Kendra said. For some reason, as I looked around at the white cabinets, bright lights and large center worktable, I thought about L.B. and Dr. Stephanova's lab. Finally, it was my turn to do something cooler than L.B.!

"Fossil finds in the field will eventually end up here. For example, this specimen." She pointed to the large fossil on the table. "We just found this hadrosaur skull fragment on the Alberta–B.C. border. We are not disclosing its location as we are concerned about fossil bandits."

Fossil bandits. Even sociopathic thieves with no morals thought dinosaurs were fascinating. Because they are.

With everybody crowded in around her, Kendra pointed to the rock so we could see the outline of the fossil fragment, and we all appreciated its magnificence.

"So, if you're all ready, we're going to head out on a bus to drive to our dig site. It is an active site that has yielded footprints. We think they may be part of a trackway but need to dig a bit more to find out definitively. At the same site, we have found several coprolites. Does anybody know what coprolites are?"

Everybody's hand flew up. An impatient boy who, based on his arrogance and rude behavior, was clearly a close cousin of Ryan's, shouted, "Dinosaur poo!"

"*Fossilized* dinosaur poo," I corrected him under my breath. Kids who don't wait their turn are the worst.

"Yes," Kendra said. "Fossilized poo!"

The room fell silent. Kendra's eyes scanned the group. "Do you think it's time to go?" she asked.

"Yes!" we all screamed.

"Okay, make sure you have all your belongings before you board the bus. I'll tell you more as we go." Kendra and her assistant gathered bags filled with the equipment we'd need for the day. "Please remember, for the next three hours, you are junior paleontologists commissioned by the Royal Tyrrell Museum."

I took a slow, focused breath and adjusted my field vest.

We filed outside of the laboratory area, using the back door reserved for paleontologists, to where a small bus waited for us. The driver opened the door and Kendra stood with her hand in the air, silently drawing our attention. It was noticeably hotter than when we had arrived in the morning.

"Before you get on the bus, I'd like to give you all something." She unzipped her backpack and pulled out a plastic bag filled with books. "They usually only give these to staff."

She smiled warmly as she walked down the line, handing each junior paleontologist a sturdy field notebook with the words "Royal Tyrrell Museum" embossed in gold lettering across the front.

I reached out for mine and then held it tightly to my chest.

"The paper is waterproof, because even when it rains, you still need to take notes in the field. Bad weather can't stop science!"

Waterproof paper. Imagine finding something so important that you needed to keep writing, even in a downpour. This was the most professional notebook I'd ever owned. My face was locked in a perpetual grin that wouldn't quit. I tucked it carefully into my bag.

I took a seat near the front so I could see everything and I tried to calm my nerves. We drove for about fifteen minutes before we reached our field study area. The ride was a bit bumpy and jarring. My teeth clomped together after the bus drove over a particularly large hole. The rough landscape bounced us around and we all had to hold on to the seats in front of us to avoid getting tossed. The tools in my vest clattered against my chest.

Grateful when the bus finally reached its destination, we still had to walk some distance to our dig site. The layered sedimentary rocks proved to be hard terrain to walk on because of the slopes and angles. I caught myself slipping a few times. A lot of the kids had to use their hands to keep their balance. I pulled my sun hat from my backpack. There was small brushy vegetation, but none of it tall enough to provide shade. Also, it was hard not to notice the heat. It was beyond hot outside. After only a short while, the brim of my hat was drenched in my own sweat. I looked down at my chest and the dinosaur on my T-shirt looked like he was swimming in a lake entirely made up of my own body juice. I pulled my shirt away from my chest and flapped it for some air.

It didn't help. But that was okay; this was real, hands-on paleontology! Science is not a fair-weather activity. I tried to stay positive.

When Kendra, who was leading from the front, finally stopped, we all gathered around her. Her assistant dropped her bag on the ground and started to unpack.

I was handed a small pick, a brush, a hammer and a chisel.

"I have my own," I told Kendra's assistant. I pointed to my vest.

She looked impressed and passed the set of tools to the next kid, who was not nearly as prepared as I was.

"Now open your field guides," Kendra said. "I'd like you to take a minute and observe your surroundings. Environmental observations are vital for good fieldwork. Take notes. Sketch a picture. Look at where we are. Think about the landscape and the space. Imagine—dinosaurs once roamed right where we are."

We all sat quietly and let it sink in. Some kids started writing right away, while others stared around at the rocks. Kendra and her assistant walked around and patiently watched us work.

I started drawing. It felt good to get my pencil going and I drew the landscape as best as I could. I wrote:

THIS IS DRUMHELLER. WHERE DINOSAURS ONCE ROAMED.

After a few minutes, Kendra spoke again. "Now that you've spent some time reflecting on the landscape and your surroundings, the next step is planning."

Some kids moaned, impatient to start excavating.

"I know, I know, you're eager to get going. But we have to stop and ask ourselves some questions. What is our purpose here today? Where will we work? What tools will we need? What is the best approach? Asking questions and finding answers are key components to being a good scientist. Thinking about what you're going to do is important. Take a few minutes, then I'll be ready to show you where you'll be digging!"

I wrote down my thoughts:

BEING A PALEONTOLOGIST REQUIRES DEEP THOUGHT AND PATIENCE.

SLOW AND CAREFUL.

LOOK AROUND.

PAY ATTENTION TO ALL THE DETAILS.

I put my pencil down and waited for Kendra.

After a few more minutes, Kendra finally stood up and said, "Are you ready?"

"Yes!" we all practically shouted.

We broke into smaller groups and were led around a small outcropping of rocks. There, hidden from view from where we'd stopped to take notes, was the live, active excavation site. For a second, I forgot how to breathe. There were grids, just like the one I had at home, placed on the ground. Fresh piles of dirt and a few leftover tools made the site seem so *real*.

Kendra and her assistant showed us how careful we had to be. It was my first time using my chisel on real rocks, and it was hard work. Exposed and layered sedimentary rock is considered one of the softer kinds of rock, much softer than metamorphic, but it may as well have been a solid diamond boulder. Chipping away at an area required laser-like focus and much more force and energy than I had anticipated. The initial buzz was wearing off. I was suddenly very tired. My shirt was still sticking to my back, making me uncomfortable.

The work was more tedious than I thought it would be. There was a lot of chipping, but no fossil finding. My muscles started to ache. I had to be so precise and couldn't just hack away at the rock, and Kendra and her assistant were watching us closely.

We became surrounded by dust the more we chipped away, and it started to mix with the dry, desertlike air. There was no breeze and the dust hovered visibly. I got a tight feeling in my chest and coughed. I stopped working and squinted up at the sun that was beating me down into a wet pulp. There wasn't a cloud in the sky. I suddenly longed for the lush air of Vancouver, filled with the sweet taste of the ocean. I imagined myself standing at the edge of Kitsilano Beach, waves lapping at my toes, gentle breezes filled with briny ocean water. It didn't help.

I started to feel wheezy. I put down my tool and reached for my bag with my water bottle. It was empty. I didn't remember drinking all my water. I coughed some more.

I patted my right pocket. Nothing. I patted my left pocket. Nothing. I patted *all* my pockets. My inhaler wasn't there. I'd been so excited this morning I couldn't remember if I had packed it and it had fallen out somewhere or if I had just plain forgotten it. Suddenly, as if somebody had smacked the back of my head with a sledgehammer, I knew where my inhaler was. It was exactly where I had left it the last time I used it—on the sofa bed in the hotel room.

Kendra came up to me and said, "Peter? Are you okay there?"

"I'm . . . fine," I managed to say through my tight chest. My throat started to feel scratchy.

"You don't sound fine." She watched me cough and wheeze for a while before she started flipping through her clipboard. "It says here that you have asthma and that you'd be bringing your own medication. Do you have your inhaler?"

I was able to shake my head. "No."

Kendra reached for her walkie-talkie. "I have a sick child. Will be returning to base."

By now, I had started to become worried. I could not catch my breath. It was the first time in years I hadn't had my inhaler with me. I lay down on the hard, crusty earth and stared up at the sky, trying to breathe calmly. In through my nose, out through my mouth. First rule of an asthma attack: don't panic. Anybody experiencing an asthma attack knows that that is easier said than done.

While I was lying there, watching clouds of dust drift by my face, I was overwhelmed by the feeling that I was a total idiot with stupid lungs and foolish dreams. I had forgotten my inhaler on the most important day of my life. My "practice excavations" hadn't prepared me for *anything*. Digging in the pit at Hammy and Haji's was *nothing* like the real thing. Not even close. Here I was looking the part with my "professional" vest full of tools, and my ridiculous socks— why did I wear the socks? I came here today confident that I was prepared. Lying on the ground gasping for air proved I was not. As my wheezing became louder and louder, I summoned up my last bit of strength and, in a rage, I threw my official field guide away, into a small scrubby bush.

Kendra gave her assistant instructions and then she helped me up off the rocks and led me back to the bus. My body was fighting with itself. I wanted to breathe so badly, but I couldn't get any air. It was like a plastic bag was covering my mouth, and no air was getting through.

"Come on, Peter. We need to get you back to your parents so they can get you an inhaler. Just try to relax." Kendra drove me back to the museum. I wheezed the entire way. I was the only kid who probably ever failed the Junior Scientist Dig.

Chapter 14

WHEN AN ASTHMATIC MEETS ANCIENT ROCK DUST

STILL THE WORST DAY EVER, 2:30 P.M.

CONDITIONS: MOOD

There they were. Mom, Dad, Hammy, Haji and L.B., who was leaning against Hammy's leg, all standing in a line. They had fake "I feel so sorry for you but I'll just pretend everything is great" smiles. I scowled. I could hardly lift my chin off my chest to look at them. My mother quickly handed me an inhaler.

I didn't even care about turning my back when I used it, like I usually did. This was just another small insult in my day. Plus, I really needed to breathe. I knew it wouldn't kick in right away, but just knowing I had the first dose in was calming. The cool mist tickled my tongue with its weird taste. It had never felt so good. The bus ride back to the museum had been the longest fifteen minutes of my life.

When I felt calmer, I ripped off my field vest and handed it to Mom. I didn't want to look at it anymore.

"You okay, Peter?" Mom asked.

I looked away and shrugged my shoulders. It was hard to talk and I wished I could have recovered without the audience.

Kendra gently put her hand on my wet and dusty back and passed me over to Mom. She gave Mom a restrained little smile. "I think he needs to take it easy for the rest of the afternoon." She handed me my Royal Tyrrell Museum field notebook, the one I had thrown into the brush. There was still a twig stuck to it. "I picked this up before we got on the bus."

I took it reluctantly. Then I inhaled my second puff. I was still wheezing, but it was quieter now. The scratchy ache in my throat was now just a tickle.

Kendra looked at me with pity in her eyes. "Peter, I hope you had a little bit of fun at least. I know you must be a real dinosaur enthusiast. Could you just wait for one second?"

I couldn't look at her. Did she really think I had *fun*? I had excavated for a total of eighteen minutes. My life's ambition has been crushed by a cloud of rock dust.

I had never felt so awful in my life. Before this, I thought Ryan scoring on me was bad. But *this*? This was a million times worse than getting scored on. My blood felt like lava.

Kendra came back, holding the latest issue of the Royal Tyrrell newsletter. "Do you know about this upcoming contest?" She pointed to the back page.

I half-nodded, half-shrugged.

"When we were having our environmental observation time, I saw that you were sketching the landscape. I love the way you showed the layers and textures of the rocks. It would be amazing if you sent me something!" She held out the newsletter for me. I refused to take it, so L.B. took it instead.

Kendra waved, turned around and spoke into her walkie-talkie while heading back to the bus.

"Peter, it's okay," Haji said gently. I couldn't look at him. He was probably so disappointed in my failure. They had built me the excavation pit at their house. They had tried to help me so much. I let him down.

He leaned over and said quietly, "Want Haji to buy you something nice from the gift shop?"

Mom rolled her eyes and said, "Dad . . ."

I hated being so weak, but the idea of him buying me something actually made me feel better. I wanted to be strong and tell him, *No! I don't need new toys! My life's dream has been shattered and you want to bribe me with material possessions?* But instead I nodded and the corners of my mouth involuntarily curved upward. I didn't think it was possible, but now I felt like even more of a pathetic weakling. I was such a loser I was going let Haji buy my happiness. I had no self-respect.

He nodded back. "Okay, anything you like," he said quietly so Mom couldn't hear.

"Anything?" I whispered back, as I could feel the oxygen coming back into me.

"Anything!" His eyes were kind and reassuring.

I played it cool. I scanned the merchandise and couldn't help but notice that they had some good stuff.

"Look at all these really amazing paleontology books, Peter! We don't have this one," Mom said, standing in front of a packed bookcase.

"I'm kind of over it," I replied.

"What do you mean?" she said, confused.

"Dinosaurs."

She stared at me. "You're *over* dinosaurs?"

"Well, I mean, I still like dinosaurs, in a general way . . . like, I'd go see the next *Jurassic World*." I took a slow breath. It wasn't deep, but it was getting there. "But I'm *never* going to be a paleontologist. Mom, you don't know how harsh the conditions are! Vancouver seems like a paradise compared to what it's like out there. The sun is brutal! The dust. There's so much dust! The chipping and brushing! And it's so dry!" I had said too much and gasped for air.

Mom tilted her head and gave me an "are you serious?" stare.

"It's just . . ." I paused, calming myself. The carpet of the gift shop was suddenly the most interesting thing I'd seen all day and I stared at it intensely. After a very long, uncomfortable pause, I glanced up. "I just didn't know it was going to be like that. It's just not for me. It seemed so cool in books, but in real life, it's lame."

Mom's face contorted: first angry, then amused and finally frustrated. She opened and closed her mouth a few times, like she was going to say something but then changed her mind, before she finally said, "So, this trip was a waste of time?"

"What? No! It wasn't a waste of time at all. At least now I know. I won't spend any more time dreaming of doing something that I can't . . . I don't want to do."

She pursed her lips. "Okay, I see your point, but . . . we should probably talk more about this later."

Haji came up behind me and asked, "So, Peter, do you see anything you like?" I hadn't had a chance to look around enough yet. I shook my head.

Everybody split up to browse on their own. I saw L.B. run to the giant bin of stuffed dinosaurs.

She picked up a mint green T. rex stuffie and yelled across the gift shop, "Hammy, look! So green, so soft!" She waved it around.

Hammy smiled at L.B. "It's cute!"

"Trixie," L.B. said loudly. She had a seriousness about her as she walked closer to where the rest of us were standing. "Combine *tyrannosaur* and *rex*. Perfect. Trixie is mine. I'm never going to let you go." She gave Trixie a large, suffocating hug.

"Put that back, L.B.," Mom said offhandedly.

"No," she said firmly. She tucked the stuffed dinosaur under her right armpit and quickly ran both of her hands up the panel of sequins on her smiling-emoji T-shirt, changing the face to a frowning emoji. I didn't even know that T-shirt had a frowning-face side!

Mom and Dad looked shocked. "L.B.!" Dad said sternly. "Your mother asked you to put that back!"

"I won't," she replied. Her face matched her T-shirt and she clutched Trixie closer to her chest.

I perked up. Oh, this was getting good. My afternoon of humiliation faded a little into the background.

My mother crouched down to look L.B. straight in the

eyes. "Put . . . that . . . back." Mom spoke slowly and deliberately, unable to hide her bubbling irritation.

I stared at the scene. It was like the best movie I had ever watched, but it had no action. It was all drama.

L.B. said nothing, but she glared at my mother and shook her head no, strongly with her jaw locked into place. It was like an old-fashioned Western showdown at high noon.

"It's a stuffed toy for *babies*," Mom said contemptuously. "It is not suitable for somebody of your abilities!"

"L.B.," Dad said, "I'm very disappointed in your immature behavior."

L.B. held her ground.

Hammy stepped in. "*Aigoo*. Let her have it. People looking." Her eyes darted around to the other customers in the gift shop who were pretending not to watch.

Mom looked at Hammy and said, "Mom, I'm not going to buy it for her! It's a silly toy. She's beyond something like this!"

"Fine. Then I'm going to!" Hammy grabbed L.B.'s hand and walked her to the cash register. "Grandparent's job is to make grandchildren happy!"

L.B. smiled and hung on tightly to Hammy.

"*My* job is to provide her with opportunities that help her reach her potential!" Mom shouted back as she brandished the *Complete Encyclopedia of Ancient Life: Ultimate Reference Guide with Subatomic Illustrations* in the air. She needed two hands because it was about six inches thick. Now lots of other shoppers were staring at us—and not even trying to pretend that they weren't.

That was the best free entertainment I'd had in weeks. I leaned in toward Haji and told him, "I'll take that, please." I pointed up to a microscope behind a locked cabinet.

He winked at me. "Sure."

Hammy stood in the checkout line to buy the dinosaur stuffie and Mom stood right behind her, practically breathing down Hammy's neck, clutching the giant textbook. When we left the gift shop, Haji passed me a large shopping bag with my new microscope, and I looked at him gratefully. It didn't make up for my terrible day, and so I did the only thing that would make me feel better—I threw my official Royal Tyrrell Museum field notebook in the garbage.

Chapter 15

MISSION: GET OUT OF DRUMHELLER

FRIDAY, JULY 5, TOO EARLY

CONDITIONS: BLAH

We had one more day in Drumheller after my terrible afternoon. One more day of being surrounded by all things dinosaur. One more day to remind me of my stupidity. One more day to remind me what a failure I was. I vowed to myself that my note-taking days were over. After today, we still had a few days of holidays, but I didn't care where else we went; I just wanted to get out of *here*.

L.B. sat on her sofa bed and read a book to Trixie. As Mom watched, she winced, as if she had developed a sudden eye tick.

"Come on. Let's all get ready to go." Dad interrupted me as I pretended to read a two-day-old newspaper that had been left in the room.

"Can I just stay in the hotel room?" I pleaded.

"No, Peter, you're coming with us," Mom insisted while packing up her purse.

"I really don't need to see anything else."

"There's the World's Largest Dinosaur statue and Mega Fossil Land!" L.B. said perkily. "The animatronic dinosaurs look quite fascinating!" She held up a pamphlet for me to see. "Audio engineers have estimated the sound the T. rex may have made and have reproduced it. People with sensitive ears are required to wear ear protection!"

"I can see the World's Largest Dinosaur from pretty much anywhere in the entire city. And I don't need to go deaf listening to a T. rex scream. I already have you in my life."

She frowned at me and crossed her arms.

"Ah, but we can climb inside!" Haji said, looking at the brochure.

"Hammy needs you to hold my hand. Stairs might be steep. I might fall." Hammy gave me her little look, the one where her eyes twinkle and she tries to look all serious, but it was more likely that she might start laughing at any time. It was the look I couldn't say no to. I put down the newspaper, defeated.

I refused to unbuckle my seat belt.

"I'll stay here with Peter until he becomes reasonable," Mom said to Dad as the rest of the family got out of the car.

She was going to be waiting forever.

She folded her arms and gave me a laser-beam stare that could have split me in two. Trying desperately to distract myself, I kicked the soccer ball at my feet. It felt deflated, just like me.

"What if Hammy falls?" Her scowl darkened.

"Mom, L.B. will be clutching her hand the entire time. Hammy will be fine. Plus, look at that thing—would I even fit inside?" I pointed to the World's Largest Dinosaur. You could see the rickety metal stairs inside the cavity of the structure even from the parking lot. "I'd probably bang my head a dozen times anyway."

She wasn't buying anything I was selling. My mother's piercing gaze was making the van seem stuffy. I needed to change the topic. I seized this moment of privacy to ask what I'd been wondering for a few days.

"Mom, what's wrong with Hammy?" No point beating around the bush.

I could see the muscles in her face tense up. She squeezed her lips together.

"I mean, I know she's getting old. I know old people can forget things or whatever, but this feels . . . different."

"Well, Peter, to be honest, we're not sure," she finally answered.

"You've seen it, though, right? All the weird stuff that's been happening with her?" I asked.

"Yes," she answered, nodding slightly.

"She keeps forgetting stuff. She called me Ji Won. I'm worried, Mom."

"We're all worried, Peter. She has a few appointments when we get back, so we'll know more later. Right now, please just try not to make a big deal about it. It's important to be patient with her."

I leaned back in my seat. "Okay."

"Do you want to go inside now?" She motioned to the giant T. rex.

"Fine." I unbuckled my seat belt.

As I got out of the car, all I could hear was the resounding echo of L.B. roaring and then giggling hysterically from inside the dinosaur.

"See, aren't you glad we waited?" I asked Mom.

Chapter 16

THE HOODOO THAT YOU DO

7:30 P.M.

CONDITIONS: SURPRISE, IT'S STILL HOT

I really just wished we could have gone straight home, but Mom and Dad insisted we continue with the rest of our itinerary as planned. After being dragged into the World's Largest Dinosaur, I was then forced to take a train ride while sitting in a converted coal cart at the Atlas Coal Mine. It was exactly as uncomfortable as it sounds.

The very last thing in Drumheller was our visit to the hoodoos. I didn't want to admit it, but they were pretty cool. They were made of the same layered sedimentary rock that was all around the badlands, but erosion had caused them to take on special shapes. Imagine big sandstone mushrooms popping up on the side of a scrubby mountain. It was like an extraterrestrial landscape, teeming with alien life (but they were actually tourists).

L.B. kept shouting, "Hoo-*dooooo!*" Over and over again. It got old pretty fast. We had to leave when she put Trixie on top of one of the solid slabs of rock protecting the soft sandstone column and she got caught by one of the park rangers. She must have missed the big "Do not touch!" signs that were *everywhere*.

"But he's a dinosaur! It's his natural habitat!" she argued with the ranger.

"Sorry, miss. Even dinosaurs aren't allowed to roam here anymore," he replied. I guess he was pretty good-natured about the whole thing, but he was still insistent we get back to the van and *leave*.

The best part was Mom's face. She was mortified. Something about the whole thing almost made me laugh. Almost.

Then, that was it. We were done with Drumheller and we could leave tomorrow. When we got back to the hotel, I packed up my suitcase and, with it, all my dreams.

SATURDAY, JULY 6, 10:30 A.M.
CONDITIONS: DRUMHELLER IN THE REARVIEW
MIRROR. TOTAL, ABSOLUTE RELIEF

We couldn't get a hotel room in Calgary because the Calgary Stampede was on. But my parents had bought tickets to the rodeo and that's where we were headed. We're from *Vancouver*. And we're *Korean*. I had never ever been anywhere where I felt out of place for not having a cowboy hat, but that is exactly how I felt at the stampede. I was sure Calgary wasn't always like this, but today I was glad we were here for only a few hours before heading to our hotel in Canmore.

We had terrible seats in the stadium because we booked everything so late, but that didn't stop L.B. from waving that silly dinosaur in the air and yelling to the contestants, "Trixie is cheering you on!" L.B. was having the time of her life and shouting "Yeehaw!" whenever it was appropriate, and often when it was not.

After watching a few barrel races, I saw Hammy talking to Mom and then Mom talking to Dad. I couldn't hear a thing.

I asked Hammy what was wrong.

"It's too exciting for me here," she replied wearily. I could see she was trying to smile, but she couldn't quite manage it.

It *was* really loud and overwhelming in the stadium.

"I'll take her to the van," I volunteered to Mom.

She looked relieved. "Thank you, Peter. L.B.'s having such a good time, it would be a shame to make her leave."

After digging around in her purse for a minute, she found her keys and handed them to me.

Hammy held my arm as we slowly walked back to the van.

So while I can tell people I've been to the Calgary Stampede, the truth is, most of my time there was spent watching Hammy sleep in the back of the minivan. She'd been a real trooper while being dragged all over Drumheller yesterday, so I hoped today she just needed a bit more sleep and would be as good as new. I was keeping my eye on her, just in case.

The parking lot at the stampede is just like any other parking lot, except for the smell. We had all the windows rolled down in the van so we didn't suffocate, and when the wind blew in a certain direction, I could sometimes not smell horse manure. This air didn't make me wheeze; it just made me dry heave, so I took that as a small victory.

At least I had a giant book to read. I flipped through the *Complete Encyclopedia of Ancient Life: Ultimate Reference Guide with Subatomic Illustrations* because the pictures were kind of awesome.

When that got boring, I played with my flat soccer ball, and I tried keeping it up in the air with my feet, but the flatness made it impossible to predict where the ball would go.

I could hardly believe that I was happy to see L.B. skipping through the parking lot. I was even happier to see Mom holding a takeout container.

"Leave some for Hammy in case she's hungry when she wakes up." Mom passed me the box.

I opened it up to see cold chicken strips and fries. Here's some math: four chicken strips between two people equals one hungry boy.

We settled into the van and everybody buckled up. Hammy roused slightly, but stayed asleep.

"Next stop Canmore," Dad said.

"Yeehaw!" L.B. yelled through her open window.

Chapter 17

CONVERT THIS

The only thing to say about Canmore was we had to stop for a moose that was crossing the road in the middle of town. That was decent. A moose is a lot bigger in real life than you'd think.

When we saw it, L.B. grabbed her book, *Four Thousand Amazing Facts to Share*, and flipped wildly until she came to the page she was looking for.

"A full-grown moose can weigh 1,300 pounds! That's . . . 590 kilograms."

I turned to stare at her.

"Don't you wish there were global standardized units for weights and measurements?" she asked me.

"Yes, I'm sure it would bring about world peace," I told her, my voice as deadpan as I could make it.

"Are you mocking me, Petey?" L.B. puckered her mouth and hugged Trixie tight.

"What do you think, Little Einstein?"

Mom gave me a dirty look and so did L.B. I stared out the window placidly, knowing that we'd be home in a few days.

3:30 P.M.

I think it would be accurate to say that ever since L.B. got Trixie, she'd pretty much been strangling that green fluff ball. Trixie's face was often smashed up against the window as we made the drive out of Alberta, back into British Columbia. In just a few days, Trixie had developed a noticeable gray ring around his neck from her grimy hands.

Our last stop before the final push home was Kelowna. At the hotel, there was an in-suite washing machine and dryer, so Mom said to L.B., "Can we at least wash that thing? He's getting a bit dirty, don't you think?"

"This?" She pointed to his gray neck. "This is the mark of true love. You may never wash Trixie."

L.B. would probably say that getting Trixie at the gift shop was the highlight of her time in Drumheller. I guess, considering how things went at the dig, the microscope Haji bought me was the best thing that happened to me in Drumheller, but the bar was pretty low, wasn't it? Normally I would have been too embarrassed to ask for such an expensive gift (I realized after he bought it that it was the priciest item in the store). I had already passed into the realm of utter and complete humiliation, though, so how could I possibly feel badly about asking for a gift that Haji was practically begging me to pick?

This was not a toy microscope; it was a serious one. Even Mom thought it was an excellent choice. "Maybe this is just the thing you need to develop an interest in molecular biology!"

I hadn't had much of a chance to use the microscope while we were in Drumheller or Canmore. In Kelowna, though, we had a few hours to just hang out. We could have gone to do some exploring, but even Mom and Dad were too tired to go for a hike at Knox Mountain, and we settled for a short walk along the waterfront before we all came back to the hotel room and crashed. Hammy was so tired she fell asleep sitting in an armchair. I pulled the small coffee table as far away from Hammy as I could and I set up the microscope.

Haji sat down to watch me and said, "*Cha*, looks very professional! You pick best thing in the gift shop."

I smiled at him and opened the lid to the box of slides

that came with the microscope. The box was neatly organized with almost two hundred different slides covering
all kinds of different branches of science. I loved this box of
slides. The interior of the box was fitted with little grooves
so that the slides fit perfectly, without touching each other.
Each slide was labeled clearly and color-coordinated by
topic. It was like a work of art.

Haji peered at the box of slides and gingerly pulled out
one of the specimens. "What's this?"

I read the label. "See how it's colored red? Red means it's
herpetology, the study of reptiles and amphibians."

Haji adjusted his glasses and read, "Chameleon skin."
He made a face.

"Poor chameleon," L.B. said sadly.

"What are the blue slides?" Haji asked.

"Biology." I lifted up a slide to show him. "This one is
a cross section of . . ." I put the slide down.

"What?" he asked.

"Dog tongue." I grimaced.

"Why is science so cruel?" L.B. cried.

Her words punched me in the gut. Science *was* cruel.
How can you *think* you love something so much and then
have it treat you so badly? Paleontology fieldwork was the
cruelest science of all.

"Do you have any slides that do not require the death of an innocent animal?" L.B. stroked Trixie's head.

"It says on the box that no animals were harmed to produce slide samples," I told her.

"I prefer to stay ignorant about their origin nonetheless!"

I looked back into the box. "Here. The green ones, botany. Here's a nice harmless slide of dandelion pollen."

"That's better," she said, looking more relaxed. "Can I see?"

I put the slide into the clips, and I was adjusting the eyepiece before I started to fine-tune the focus when I saw a flash of fluffy mint green fabric. L.B. had stuck Trixie's stubby little arm under the lens.

"Hey! Quit it!" I yelled while I batted Trixie away from my microscope.

"I was just wondering if Trixie had any visible bacteria," L.B. said.

I looked up from the eyepiece. "You've been holding that *thing* for four days straight. It's been to the washroom with you. It's fallen on the ground in a park. It's been to several restaurants. Remember when you were at the playground in Canmore and you shoved him down the front of your shorts so you could do monkey bars? I think it's a pretty good guess to say yes, Trixie is full of bacteria."

"Beneficial bacteria or harmful bacteria?" she said. "There is a marked difference." She tried to push his arm under the lens again.

"L.B., stop it! This is fragile! I thought you wanted to see the pollen slide."

"I changed my mind."

"That stupid dinosaur has *every* kind of bacteria! Now leave me alone!"

"Sh! Hammy's trying to sleep!" Mom hissed at us.

"We need to get home, like, yesterday," Dad said, rubbing his forehead. He stuck his fingers under his glasses and massaged his eyes. "Both of you, stop it! Do *not* wake up your grandmother!"

I stared at Hammy; she hadn't moved and was snoring softly.

"We're all vacationed out," Mom said. "Could you two *please* stop arguing? Give each other some space!"

Mom turned to Dad and said, "I can't wait to get back to our regular routines. I'm sure L.B. has been away from her math tutor for too long." He nodded in agreement.

L.B. frowned deeply and clutched Trixie even closer to her.

We retreated to our separate corners. Dad was right; we needed to get home. I was sick of sharing a washroom with so many other people. I was so tired of sitting in the van. I hadn't punched a soccer ball away from the net for too long now and actually almost, kind of, missed seeing Ryan's face when he didn't score. But, in a weird way, this road trip had taught me a couple of important things. First, I was *done* with paleontology. Second, something was definitely wrong with Hammy and I was going to find out more.

Chapter 18

PACIFIC BREEZES ARE
THE BEST BREEZES

MONDAY, JULY 8, 5:20 P.M.

CONDITIONS: CLIMATE-CONTROLLED. WILLIS

CARRIER, INVENTOR OF AC, IS MY HERO

We left Kelowna after eating an early lunch, and Dad busted down the highway like a man who was on a mission to end the holiday as soon as possible. Two hours later Mom took the wheel and she weaved in and out of traffic with mad skills. I didn't know the minivan could move like that. When we took the off-ramp and I saw the "Welcome to Vancouver" sign, it felt like a giant relief.

"Almost there," Dad said. "We're going to drop Haji and Hammy off first."

I looked over at my grandparents. Both of them had their eyes closed. I didn't know if they were sleeping or just resting. Haji sat upright in his seat, but Hammy had folded up a sweater and used it like a pillow to put her head against the window.

The sight of the city made me feel happy and, for the last stretch of the drive, we drove in complete silence. No Korean audiobook, no talking, no music. Just quiet. I think we all needed it. Mom even relaxed a bit and stopped driving like somebody was chasing us.

We turned the corner and everything seemed so familiar and yet so strange at the same time. The neighborhood I knew so well I suddenly saw with fresh eyes. Little details that I had missed I now noticed. That house on the corner of Boundary Road and Joyce Street, was it always yellow?

I counted off the streets as we passed them. Monmouth. Wellington. Yardley. The next one was Hammy and Haji's. It was their same old house, and everything looked normal, but it felt different. Maybe I was different.

When Mom slowed down and parked, everybody in the entire van relaxed. You could actually feel all the muscles in everyone's body just kind of give way.

Mom pressed the button, and the side door slid open. I squeezed between Hammy and Haji's seats and jumped out of the van. Haji stirred and then finally realized he was home. He got out of the van stiffly and stretched his back.

He patted my shoulder as I stood by the van door waiting for Hammy.

Hammy didn't move. L.B. leaned forward and stroked Hammy's arm. "Hammy," she whispered in her ear. "You're home."

Her eyes opened slowly and she looked like she was trying to focus her gaze. "What? Where are we?"

"Home," L.B. answered.

"Oh, oh," she said. "Thank you, Charlotte." Hammy patted L.B.'s cheek, collected her handbag and got out of the car. L.B. followed her.

My mouth fell open instantly. L.B.'s eyes darted toward mine. Our eyes locked for a second before we looked over at our parents, who hadn't heard.

Neither of us said anything. We just stood outside the van, slightly stunned, watching our parents get Hammy and Haji's bags out of the car.

"Peter, don't just stand there. Help!" Mom said, irritated.

Startled, I grabbed the handle of a suitcase and rolled it inside the house. L.B. remained by the van with her eyebrows scrunched and her lips pursed.

When the last bag was unloaded, we all stood around and said, "Well . . ."

"Good trip!" Haji said, shaking Dad's hand and leaning in for a hug from Mom.

"Yes, yes," Hammy said. "Wonderful sightseeing!" She looked at each of us and took turns giving us a hug, one by one.

"L.B. and Peter have lots of good memories from trip," Haji said.

"Well, *mostly* good memories!" Hammy laughed. She did a cute thing with her eyes, darting a glance at me but pretending not to. Everyone laughed with her. Even I tried to laugh at myself, and I forced a little, half-hearted smile. I tried for Hammy, but I had to admit that it was hard to find humor in personal failure.

L.B. gave Hammy an extra-long hug before we all got into the van for the very short drive back to our house. I looked back at Haji and Hammy for as long as I could, until I couldn't see them anymore. In just a minute, we were home too.

"Finally, we're home!" Mom said as she turned off the engine.

"Oh, I was unprepared for the euphoric feeling of familiar sights." L.B. sighed. "I feel overwhelmed! Trixie, welcome home!" She faced Trixie toward the front door, so he could see our house. I rolled my eyes and shook my head.

When Dad unlocked and opened the front door, we discovered there was a huge pile of junk mail inside, sitting underneath the mail slot. We had to give the mail a push with the weight of the door so we could get inside, stepping over all the flyers and ads.

"Peter, can you pick all this up?" Dad said to me while motioning to the ground.

There were a few large envelopes in addition to the junk mail. I was starting to sort through things when my mother came into the house, wheeling a suitcase.

"What's that?" she said abruptly.

"The mail," I answered.

She snapped the neat pile of mail out of my hands, quickly picked out the large envelopes and then handed the flyers and junk back to me. "Recycle those, please," she said. She stuffed the large envelopes into the front pouch of her suitcase. I looked at Mom curiously, which she just ignored, and I continued on into the house. I dumped the pile of paper into the recycling box before going back outside and lugging my duffel bag out of the back of the car. Then I climbed back in the van and I cleaned up around my seat—my games, my DoodleBoard. I tossed my deflated soccer ball onto the front lawn. I saw the tip of the journal I had started at the beginning of the road trip. I reached into the back pocket of the seat and pulled it out. Without looking at it, I shoved it into the duffel bag before I took it upstairs to my room. Everything that reminded me of Drumheller was zipped up tight.

Chapter 19

A RARE EVENT

I was in my room when L.B. knocked on the door. We had been back from our trip for a few days and I had quickly settled into a summertime routine of being deathly bored but also being afraid to say anything because my parents were always ready with math exercises, spelling tests or other cruel reminders of school. I found it best to stay in my room as much as possible and pretend I was reading, even if I was sometimes doing a little mindless doodling.

"What is it?" I yelled. I gathered up my papers and pushed them under my blanket.

"Petey?" L.B. asked. "Can I come in?"

"Fine . . . ," I muttered as I got up and opened the door. "What do you want?"

She shrugged her shoulders. "My coding project is done. My math tutor canceled class today because he's sick. I have free time!"

Even though I had just cracked open the door, she still managed to squeeze herself effortlessly inside, and before I knew it, she was making herself comfortable. L.B. sat down on the side of my bed and heard the crinkly sound of paper.

"What's this?" She lifted up the blanket and pulled out the one piece of paper I hadn't wanted her to see.

Her face lit up.

"It's Trixie! A modernist rendition, but you've captured his spirit!"

I tried to rip the paper out of her hands, but she was playing keep-away. She was too small and too fast.

"Petey! Why don't you want me to see this? It's so charming!" she said as she leaped off my bed and darted around my room.

"L.B.!" I shouted. "It's private!" I finally managed to grab the paper from her hands, and it ripped in two. Trixie had been decapitated.

I stared at her angrily.

"I'm sorry, Petey," she said, looking down at the half she was holding.

I crumpled up the other half and threw it toward the recycling box. It hit the side and bounced in.

She flattened out the paper on her thigh and took another look. "Where is Trixie going?"

I had drawn Trixie standing next to a bus stop.

"Dinosaur school!" I said sarcastically. I hoped that she would think I was joking when I was, in fact, not joking.

163

"Does Trixie have parents?" she asked.

"I don't know, L.B. It's your dinosaur."

She nodded. "Yes, Trixie *does* have parents."

"Whatever, L.B. Can you leave now?"

"Trixie's parents are *huge*. They are angry dinosaurs. They don't let Trixie have any fun! They make him take the bus even though he's too young to be out by himself. They want him to only eat Triceratops meat, when he wants to try vegetation for once!" L.B. had a wild expression in her eyes.

"What on Earth are you talking about?"

"Do you have paper, Petey?"

I rummaged around on my desk and wordlessly handed her a stack of paper.

"And a pencil."

"Of course," I replied, exasperated.

She dropped to the floor and laid down on her stomach. She drew a long rectangle and divided it into four boxes. She wrote "Trixie's Day Out" at the top in her messy printing and started drawing.

She stopped after she drew an outline. It had the shape of the poo emoji.

"What is that?"

"Trixie," she replied.

She was a horrible artist—like, truly wretched. I took a deep, cleansing breath and tried to suppress my emerging grin.

"Petey," she said as she put down her pencil. "I cannot draw Trixie. In my mind's eye, I see him perfectly. I cannot transfer the picture from my mind to this piece of paper. Frustrating!" She crumpled up the paper and threw it into the recycling box. *Swoosh.*

"What are you trying to draw?"

"A cartoon. Trixie wants to go wander around the Cretaceous jungle, playing with other dinosaurs, maybe playing headbutt the tree or just swinging from a branch for fun, but his parents won't let him. 'Trixie, you need to practice your roaring!' 'Trixie, you need to perfect the most efficient way to rip the Coelophysis's arm out of its socket!'" she said, pretending to be an adult T. rex.

"The Coelophysis was not alive at the same time as the T. rex. It lived during the Triassic period." I tried hard to contain my satisfaction. I couldn't believe how good I was feeling right now.

L.B. rolled her eyes. "It's just a cartoon, Petey."

"I just think that if you're going to do a dinosaur cartoon, it's got to be scientifically and chronologically accurate."

I grabbed a piece of paper and drew out squares across the full length. They were not symmetrical boxes; instead, the different squares were different sizes to make it look more interesting.

I wrote "Trixie's Day Out" in my fancy font across the top. I saved that writing for cover pages of school reports.

"How about this?" I said as I started to draw Trixie in the first square. "What's he doing?"

"Dinosaur math."

"Okay, so he's hunched over a desk, like this?" I asked. I erased and corrected his body position.

"Yes." She grinned. "Perfect."

"Now what?"

"Trixie's mom and dad come into the room, and they say, 'Four more sheets of work for you or you get no meat tonight!'" she bellowed.

I laughed. "Okay, give me a second." I thought about what Trixie's parents might look like.

As I sketched and erased and redrew, L.B. said, "The dad needs glasses." I drew them in. Then we both took a long look and erupted into giggles. It was our dad. But he was a dinosaur.

"Do Trixie's grandparents!" L.B. urged enthusiastically,

pointing at the paper. Our laughter had started to calm down and we wiped tears from our eyes.

I thought for a minute before I started to draw my best dinosaur Haji and Hammy. I asked, "What should they be doing?"

"Can you make Trixie hug dino Hammy?" she asked quietly. "Trixie is whispering in her ear that everything is going to be okay."

I nodded somberly. "I'll do my best."

Chapter 20

DEFYING THE LAWS
OF PHYSICS

Of all the months, August is the best. First, every August during the B.C. Day long weekend there is a big Korean-Canadian celebration in Central Park in Burnaby. Haji gets to wear his favorite baseball hat with the Korean and Canadian flags intertwined, Hammy waves a Korean flag around, and there is the smell of Korean BBQ in the air. It's like the best perfume. We have never missed a single one of these days for as long as I can remember. More importantly, and the real reason August is the best month, is that my birthday is on August eleventh. This year, I'll be eleven on August eleventh. That number combination will never happen again, so it's got to be lucky, right?

On Saturday, we all got up early for the festival. We

always arrived early because parking filled up fast. At the edge of the park, lots of vendors were still setting up. Even though it was only ten o'clock, I saw the Hurricane Potato truck and they looked ready for business. I asked Mom for some cash.

She looked at me with disbelief. "We just got here! You want to start eating already?"

"That's kind of the whole point, isn't it? Plus, there's no line right now!"

"Well, if you're going to get one, I'm partial to the Parmesan cheese flavor," L.B. said.

"I'm not sharing."

"Fine, get two." Mom handed me ten dollars from her wallet. I grinned because we all knew that L.B. would eat almost none of hers and then Mom would be "forced" to eat the leftovers rather than "waste" it. Who didn't like a spiral-cut potato, skewered, deep-fried and sprinkled with flavorings? It was like one long, continuous potato chip that kept on giving.

"Parmesan!" L.B. yelled back to me as Mom dragged her to a booth hosted by a bank that was giving away prizes if you threw a beanbag into a small center hole in a box. If you missed, you got a magnet. Hammy, Haji and Dad went with them, leaving me alone to get my snack.

After I had ordered a Parmesan potato and a Cajun spice for me, I stood waiting by the truck.

"Hey, Peter."

Samuel said something to his mom and then headed in my direction. I smiled and started to wave, but realized that seemed too enthusiastic, so I just held my hand up without moving it around like an idiot.

"How's your summer going?" Samuel looked relaxed and casual. I had never seen him in sandals before. I tried not to look at his toes. Other people's toes were sometimes freaky.

I shrugged. "Okay. You?"

"Pretty boring." He shrugged back. "Hey, the taekwondo show's on soon. You gonna watch?"

"I wouldn't miss it!"

"Those guys are dope," he said. "We watch every year."

"Us too!"

My potatoes were ready and I awkwardly held up the two long, spirally potatoes on sticks. I couldn't eat mine while holding L.B.'s at the same time—it would make too big a mess.

"Well, I'd better go," he said. "My *halmoni* wants to go to the *mandu* lady. She puts this special sauce on top and I could eat, like, twenty of them."

"There's a *mandu* lady?" A few little dumplings would go really well with a Hurricane Potato!

"Yeah, down in the far corner." He gestured to the end of the field. "I'll catch you later, okay?"

"Bye," I said. I headed toward the tent where my parents were trying to get free junk.

L.B. saw me and ran up to get her Hurricane Potato. Her hands were full of Frisbees. "Yum!" she said as she dropped the Frisbees and grabbed the stick.

"Why do you have so many Frisbees?" I asked. I took a bite, but it was so hot I had to keep my mouth open to let the steam escape.

"I won them."

"All of them?" I couldn't hide my surprise.

"Yes. They found it hard to believe that I could keep hitting the bull's-eye each time and kept goading me to do it again." She took a careful bite of the hot potato. "I showed them." She winked.

I rolled my eyes.

"I'm not sure what I'm going to do with all these Frisbees, though . . ."

The highlight of the entire day is the Kukkiwon Taekwondo Demonstration Team show. They come from Seoul every year to perform.

"The best part? It's free!" Dad always says that. He said the same thing last year and the year before that too. I wonder sometimes if he's actually proud of being a cheapskate.

The show is like watching a martial arts movie in real time. No editing, no CGI. If you saw the team members walking around, you'd never guess that they were martial artists extraordinaire—Korean Clark Kents. Ordinary-looking guys who could do some superhuman things. I get a weird feeling in the pit of my stomach every time I watch them.

Central Park is mostly a massive urban green space, but it also has a miniature golf course, an outdoor swimming pool, a playground area and a stadium. The stadium was built for sporting events, but they use the space for festivals too. The taekwondo team always performs in the center of the stadium, near the covered bleachers. They had a large area of red and blue foam mats set up for the show.

"Come on," Mom urged, looking at her watch. "Let's get our seats. It's filling up fast."

We liked to sit near the back, so we could be in the shade.

I patted my right pocket for my inhaler before I sat down on the stadium benches and, just out of habit, I patted my left pocket too. I shook my head, angry at myself. I had stopped carrying my notebook around, but some habits are hard to break. I didn't like to think about it too much.

I watched the crowd fill the seats. Lots of non-Koreans even came to watch. That always made me feel proud, like other people actually appreciated Korean things too. I looked around the stadium at all the people trying to find the best seat they could, jostling and forcing a lot of people who were already seated to bend their knees awkwardly so they could pass.

To my complete horror, I saw Ryan. Ryan Gagnon. Here. At a Korean festival. I'd recognize those stupid bangs anywhere. How dare he enter my domain! He was wearing a track jacket that said "Kee's Martial Arts Studio" on the back. I sank into my seat and prayed to all the world deities that he wouldn't see me. I watched him casually looking around and then, in slow motion, our eyed locked. I sat up straighter because now wasn't the time to slouch. I gave him my best death-glare laser eyes. Because I had the higher seat, he had to turn around first.

At precisely eleven thirty, an announcer in a suit and tie took to the stage and loud music came through the speakers.

He said, "And now, all the way from Seoul, the world-famous Kukkiwon Taekwondo Demonstration Team! Please give them a big round of applause!"

While trying to stare Ryan down, I had fallen into a trance-like state of intensity and the announcement suddenly reminded me about the real reason I was sitting here. I could resume hating Ryan when the show was all done.

About twenty men and two women ran out from underneath the stadium seats. They were wearing matching white *dobok* uniforms with black belts tied tightly around their waists. The word *Kukkiwon* was stitched in bold black letters across their backs. They formed a line and started clapping to the music, encouraging us to join.

The whole audience clapped for a while, but when the music changed and they broke their line to start the show, we all fell silent.

They split off into groups and lined up at the four corners of the mats laid out on the ground. As an introduction, one by one, they flew across the mats, punching, kicking and twisting through the air. Backward flips, forward flips and handsprings. Each team member performed a unique trick. They moved in elaborate, highly choreographed poses across the mats, sometimes as a large group, sometimes just showcasing one performer. After just a few minutes, they already had us all on the edges of our seats.

When the wooden boards came out, the action got even more intense. The boards are slotted into prongs on the top end of thin poles over ten feet high and you don't even notice them being carried onto the mats because there is so much going on and your eyes can't keep up with all the activity on the sides. One of the performers would use their teammates like springboards and leap off somebody's thigh or from interlocked fingers. Sometimes they didn't even need any-body else and they would just launch up to do an impossibly high jump and kick the board with their feet, do a backflip and land perfectly.

Sometimes they set up multiple poles and one of the performers kicked all of them with *one* continuous long jump. *Crack, crack, crack, crack.*

"I want to do that!" L.B. shrieked as she dug her nails into my forearm.

Then one of them put on a blindfold. A blindfold! One person rang a bell and held an apple on a stick. The blind-folded performer listened intently and adjusted his feet to ready himself. He let out a roar so ferocious I thought the apple would burst from the power of his scream. He flew into a giant roundhouse kick and smashed the apple into a pulp with the top of his foot. Juice sprayed onto the first four rows of the audience.

During the entire show, my family gasped, clutched their chests or grabbed each other's arms. It was a blur of scissor kicks, ax kicks, elbow strikes and backfists. Bodies sailed through the air sideways, upside down, straight up and in circles. Shattered pieces of wooden boards littered the stadium ground.

The end of the show was Haji's favorite part. The team did this part every year. They ran out with Korean and Canadian flags and waved them around all while dancing and weaving in and out of intricate formations. Haji would sit up straight and adjust his Korean-Canadian baseball cap proudly. The audience clapped in beat to the music.

When they finished, we all stood up and applauded until our hands were raw, cheering so loudly our throats were hoarse. My family finally sat down to collect our things. I felt drained having just witnessed an intense display of awesome Koreanness.

Each one of these amazing Korean performers had fully mastered every single law of motion. They even did things that they should not have been able to do. Their ability to control their center of mass and their mastery of kinetic energy blew my mind. And, really, the coolest thing of all was that after they'd finish their performance, they would probably go put on some sneakers and eat some rice and kimchi for lunch.

"*Cha!*" Haji said. "Amazing!" He shook his head in disbelief.

L.B. sighed and looked happy. "Oh, they looked so free."

Hammy tapped my leg. "Peter, you should try taekwondo lesson. Good for all Korean boys."

I stopped cold and so did L.B. I snuck a peek over at my parents, but they were talking to each other and not paying attention.

I *had* taken taekwondo lessons. For three years. Hammy and Haji were the ones who had taken me every week. I was having a bad asthma day when I took my last belt test. I couldn't catch my breath after the board-breaking component. I asked if I could rest and Master refused to let me take a break. Hammy stood up from the seating area and yelled at him in Korean for quite some time. To this day I don't know what she said to him, but after she sat down, he reluctantly let me get my inhaler and take a short break.

That story is a legend in my house.

"Hammy," I said tentatively. "Remember, I used to take taekwondo lessons. I have my orange belt."

She looked confused. "Oh, really?"

I looked over at L.B. and she grimaced. Then she reached over and held Hammy's hand. I caught sight of Ryan standing up, casually staring at me with his malevolent, dastardly, criminal-in-the-making eyes while walking out of the stadium with his parents and other kids wearing the same jacket as him. The day that started off with such crispy deliciousness ended with a bad taste in my mouth.

Chapter 21

TOO GROGGY TO REPORT

I thought I was having a dream, but when the ringing wouldn't stop, I forced my eyes open. Our telephone was ringing. I heard the answering machine pick up. From downstairs, I heard Mom's cell ringtone, Beethoven's *Moonlight Sonata*. Then it stopped. Next I heard Dad's cell phone; his ringtone was the first few bars of "New York, New York." Then it stopped. I was groggy and not sure if I was imagining it all.

When the landline went off again, I was almost awake. I rolled over and looked at the clock. Ugh. I heard one of my parents walking down the hall. Then I heard voices.

My bedroom door cracked open, letting a ribbon of light into my room.

"Peter," Mom said softly.

"I'm up, I'm up," I mumbled as I squinted my eyes and looked at her. She was fully dressed, in sweatpants and a hoodie. Her hair was uncombed.

"I have to go to the hospital. Hammy's been in an accident," she said.

I sat up. "Is she okay?"

"I don't know. It was the police on the phone. They just told me to go to the hospital. She was in a car accident," she said with a worried sound in her voice.

"Is Haji hurt too?"

"No, Haji wasn't with her."

"What was she doing in a car so late at night?" I was confused.

"We don't know, Peter. All we know is, she took the car by herself."

"But Hammy hardly ever drives! Especially not at night!"

"I have no answers right now," Mom said wearily.

"Should I get dressed?" I asked as I kicked the blankets off.

"It's one thirty in the morning. Your dad and I are going to pick up Haji and go to the hospital. You stay home with L.B. You're almost eleven now and this is an emergency. When L.B. wakes up, can you make her breakfast? I'm counting on you, Peter. One of us will be back as soon as we can, but I don't know how long that will be." Her voice started to quake.

"Okay." I wondered how L.B. was going to take the news.

Dad popped his head into my room and whispered, "Bye. We'll be back as soon as we can. Thank you for taking care of L.B." He turned to walk down the hall and then abruptly turned around, came into my room and quickly gave me a hug.

I hugged him back. I listened to them close the front door and watched their car drive away into the night from my bedroom window. I sat in the dark for a moment before I flicked the light switch.

I was wide awake now. I didn't know what to do. The feeling of worry was practically choking me. I reached for my inhaler. What happened to Hammy? I pursed my lips tight and, as I paced back and forth in my room, the lens on the microscope that Haji had bought me in Drumheller caught the light and refracted brightly.

Memories of our road trip started to flash through my mind. Suddenly, I wanted to see my journal of *Environmental Observations* from our trip. I needed to reread all of the notes I had taken while observing Hammy. As quietly as I could, I dug out the journal that I had left in the bottom of my duffel bag.

I flipped through the pages; my last entry was written when we were in Drumheller, almost three weeks ago. I had stopped writing in journals since . . . giving up paleontology. I started thinking about Hammy. What had I missed? There were days when she forgot little things, but then there were days she was *fine*. I felt stupid, because she clearly wasn't fine. Some "scientist" I was—I had done a terrible job observing and recording information about Hammy. I didn't deserve to be a paleontologist anyway.

I wondered how L.B. could have slept through all that phone ringing. I crossed the hallway, quietly opened the door to her room and peered inside. She was sound asleep, with Trixie tucked under her arm. What was I going to tell her in the morning?

I worried L.B. would wake up before me if I went to bed and fell asleep. Our parents weren't home. I was in charge. So I decided I had to be there right when she woke up. I grabbed my blanket and pillow and settled in for a long night sleeping on her floor.

7:05 A.M.

I woke up screaming. L.B. was staring at me, her face uncomfortably close. She was sitting cross-legged next to me on the floor of her bedroom, with Trixie sitting on her lap.

"Good morning, Petey," she said with an air of curiosity.

"You scared me." I propped myself up on one elbow.

"May I ask why you are sleeping in this unusual spot?"

"L.B." I rubbed my eyes to wake myself up. "Nobody else is home."

She looked surprised. "What do you mean?"

"They had to go to the hospital last night to see Hammy. There's been an accident," I said cautiously but clearly.

She gasped.

"I don't know anything, so please don't ask me," I said, feeling helpless.

Fortunately, we heard the front door open and, like a rocket, L.B. ran out of her room.

"Hammy?!" she shouted. I got up and trailed her.

It was Dad.

"L.B., Peter, you're up," he said tiredly, taking off his jacket.

"Is Hammy okay?" L.B. demanded.

"L.B., calm down. Have a seat."

"How can I possibly be calm?" L.B. practically screamed. I thought she was going to rip Trixie apart she was so worked up.

Dad sighed heavily. "Hammy is okay, but she's pretty banged up."

"I have to see her *now!*" L.B. wailed.

I breathed deeply, relieved that she was alive.

"L.B., she is in no shape to see you right now. She is heavily medicated and wouldn't even know you were there," Dad said as gently as he could.

L.B. collapsed on the floor.

7:10 A.M.

Dad called 911. I stared at my sister lying on the ground. My heart was racing and I held my fingertips up against her nose to make sure she was still breathing. She was. Because it is what they do in the movies, I also felt her wrist for a pulse.

"Peter! Is she breathing?" Dad was kneeling right next to me, but his voice was loud and frantic.

I nodded.

"Yes!" he told the operator. He covered the mouthpiece of the phone, leaned into me and said, "They're sending an ambulance."

That's when L.B.'s eyes popped open and, wide-eyed, she looked at me and then at Dad, who dropped the phone.

"Petey, we have to stop meeting this way," L.B. said. It was the strangest thing that could have come out of her mouth. But she was back and I felt relieved.

Dad, who by this time was sweating profusely, practically shouted, "What on Earth is she talking about?"

I shook my head. "It's a long story."

7:45 A.M.

The taller, blond male paramedic asked L.B. questions and checked her eyes and pulse. He turned to his female partner and they consulted each other before he said, "We think she fainted from shock."

"Actually, the correct term is *vasovagal syncope*," L.B. corrected as she sat up. She picked a fine time to be obnoxious.

The paramedics broke into huge smiles at her. How could they not? They probably thought it was cute to be so small and know ridiculous things like that. Plus, she was still wearing her pajamas with the hamburger-and-fries pattern that Hammy had bought for her. The whole package must have just seemed so *adorable*.

"You can take her to the hospital if you want to be extra safe, but it's probably okay if you just keep her home and monitor her for the rest of the day," the female paramedic said as she packed up her things.

"Thank you, thank you," Dad mumbled as they left the house. His hair was sticking up, his shirt was sticking out. It looked like he was going to be the next one to need medical assistance.

Mom phoned again, and I picked up.

"How's L.B.?" she frantically shouted.

"The paramedics just left. She's fine. They think she just fainted from shock."

"Vasovagal syncope!" L.B. said, sipping the water Dad had brought her. Trixie was in her lap.

"Now is not the time to be picky about terminology!" I said, exasperated.

Dad collapsed on the sofa with his forearm covering his eyes.

"Did she just correct you?" I could hear my mom sobbing.

"Yes."

"L.B.'s going to be just fine."

"How's Hammy?" I asked.

"No change. I'll try to come home later."

"When can I see Hammy?" L.B. yelled.

"Tell her not yet," Mom instructed me.

"Mom says not yet," I told her.

L.B. pouted.

"Peter," Mom continued, "can L.B. hear me? You know she has ears like a bat."

"Just wait." I walked away from L.B. "I'm upstairs now."

"Peter, I want to tell you something. Remember when you asked me in Drumheller what was wrong with Hammy? Well, we knew she was having trouble with her memory, but it's a lot more serious than we realized. I hesitated to tell you then because I didn't want you kids to worry. But now with the accident . . . the doctors want to keep her in the hospital for a while to do some more tests. I've been thinking a lot, and I don't think L.B. can handle this situation . . . emotionally." She paused. I breathed heavily into the phone. "She's just so attached to Hammy . . ."

"I know," I whispered.

"Peter, if L.B. asks about Hammy, change the subject or be optimistic, okay?"

I scrunched my brow. I didn't like lying to L.B., but I didn't want her to faint again either.

"Okay, I'll try," I promised.

"Good. See you later."

I carried the phone back downstairs and L.B. was standing at the bottom of the stairs waiting for me.

"What else did you and Mom talk about?"

I paused. "She wanted me to make sure you were keeping on top of your math exercises and that you didn't forget your homework for your programming class." I was shocked at how easy that was. That sounded totally like Mom.

She scowled at me. "Unbelievable! Hammy is in the hospital and she continues to worry about my *enrichment*. Where are her priorities?"

Chapter 22

LET THERE BE CAKE

MONDAY, AUGUST 12, 5:30 P.M.

CONDITIONS: FAIRLY BLEAK

My eleventh birthday came and went. Nobody said anything. No one. Mom, Dad and Haji had been busy the last few days with Hammy—so busy that everybody forgot my birthday. All day yesterday, I felt a prickly sensation waiting for somebody to acknowledge me in some way, but the day passed and, when there was nothing, I felt numb. For the first few hours of the day, I wanted to drop a hint or point to the calendar, but I didn't because the thought of me complaining about nobody remembering my birthday made me feel like a giant turd. Hammy was hurt and her recovery was more important than my birthday, so I shrugged it off as best as I could.

Joe didn't even send me a text or anything! But then I remembered we were dudes and we didn't do that kind of thing. After my lousy July, I really didn't think August could be any worse, but I had never been so wrong. So much for August being the best month.

At home, there was really nothing else to talk about except Hammy. Mom updated us on Hammy's progress each night, since L.B. and I weren't allowed to see her while she was in the hospital. L.B. tried everything to get Mom to change her mind. She tried using reasonable arguments like "Hammy would be pleased to see her only granddaughter." Mom shook her head *no*. She tried whining, "I *need* to see her! Why won't you let me see her?" Mom shook her head *no*. She tried begging, "You are so mean! *Please* can I see her?" Mom shook her head *no*. L.B. finally gave up and sent a substitute instead. "Can you please take Trixie to her?" Mom finally nodded *yes*.

"Hammy knows how much you love Trixie. I'm sure this will mean a lot to her." This morning, Mom took Trixie to see Hammy at the hospital and L.B. was left with two big holes in her life.

L.B. seemed different, quieter. When she wasn't seeing her math tutor or doing her online computer programming course, she mostly sprawled herself on the carpet and stared at the ceiling. Mom hadn't signed me up for anything this summer, so I did a little bit of that too. Some days I didn't even feel like playing *Asteroid Cataclysm* on my tablet.

It was a chaotic time for my parents and so I guess I shouldn't have been surprised that nobody bothered to look at the calendar or paid attention that my birthday had passed. It was all Mom and Dad could do to make sure one of them had ordered takeout so at least we'd have some kind of a dinner.

Today at dinner—the day after I turned eleven—we were all sitting around quietly eating pizza when Haji slowly turned around, looked at the calendar and slapped his knee.

"Peter!" he exclaimed. "We all forgot."

That wasn't entirely true, but I kept my mouth shut.

L.B. looked at the calendar and then burst into tears.

Mom and Dad's faces were both frozen in horror.

"It's okay," I tried to reassure everybody. "You've been busy." I looked at the empty seat at the table.

Dad suddenly stood up. "If I hurry, I can still make it to the Chinese bakery on Kingsway!" He scrambled for his wallet and keys.

"No, Dad, it's okay." I tried to stop him. "You can get a cake tomorrow."

"I'm getting a cake right now!" He ran out the door.

Mom reached for my hand. "I'm so sorry, Peter." Tears welled up in her eyes.

I shrugged. "Really, it's okay!"

"Hammy would have remembered," L.B. said quietly. She added, "If she were here."

"Tomorrow! I take you shopping!" Haji declared. "I buy you something nice!"

"No, no. You already bought me that microscope."

"I buy you something else," he said definitively.

We were cleaning up plates and cups when my dad rushed through the door with a cake box in his hand.

"Just made it before they closed!" he said, smiling. "They only had strawberry left, but you like strawberry, right?"

I didn't say anything, but Hammy always got me a mango cake.

Dad cut the ribbon and opened up the box. "Come on!" he yelled in frustration.

"What? What's wrong?" we all said at the same time.

Dad slowly held the cake out for us to see and said, "They were not happy to help me two minutes before closing."

My cake said "Happy Birthday Pity."

"I thought it would be cute if they wrote *Petey*," Dad said, distressed. "I wrote it down for them, but I guess they couldn't read my printing."

"There is something tragic about this cake," L.B. declared with a frown.

"Let's eat it and forget it," Haji said.

"Good idea. Candles?" Mom asked Dad hopefully.

He slapped his forehead.

Suddenly, Haji started singing loudly, "Happy birthday to you!" The rest of the family joined in, but it was a pathetic chorus.

After they all stopped singing, I'm not sure what got into me—maybe it was listening to my tone-deaf family or maybe it was my misspelled name—but I leaned over and blew out imaginary candles on the cake as dramatically as I could muster. I pretended that the whole cake was covered in candles and I just blew all over the darn thing. My spit flew everywhere.

"That was the strangest thing I've ever witnessed. It's also a horrible way to spread germs needlessly," L.B. said.

"It's my belated birthday! I can do what I want!"

My parents looked at each other, confused.

I grabbed a fork and didn't wait for Mom to cut the cake. I just started eating. I started with the word *Pity*. I stabbed it and lifted a chunk of cake right out so that the word, piped in chocolate, disappeared. "Well, come on," I said with my mouth full. I chewed the *P* and *I* and *T* and *Y* as forcefully as I could. I motioned to the cake and the rest of my family joined in. Mom tentatively stabbed her fork into the whipped-cream edge. She held the piece of cake near her mouth, hesitating. I don't know why he did it, but Dad pushed her elbow and the cake missed her mouth and hit the side of her face. And that was it. We all exploded into giggles and ate like we hadn't had a meal in a week.

L.B. didn't even use a fork; she just dug her fingers right in. "We should break with convention more often!" L.B. said gleefully.

It was the first fun we'd had since Hammy's accident. My face had forgotten how to smile and it felt good to laugh again.

After the cake was mashed up and mostly eaten, I helped clean up. The recycling box next to the back door was too full to handle the cake box, so I quietly put on Mom's outdoor slippers and headed to the garage to put the recycling into the large bags the city gives us for weekly collection.

I tried picking up a wad of random cardboard and paper and jamming it into the bag, but everything just tumbled out of my arms.

"Argh!" I yelled; the sound of my own voice echoed around me in the garage. The mail that my mom had received after we got back from Drumheller caught my eye. And that envelope she'd received as a special Saturday delivery months ago. I looked through the recycling. More brochures, booklets and pamphlets I had never seen before. I flipped through them. Mom had marked some of the pages up with a highlighter. She had circled key phrases like *twenty-four-hour nursing care, private or semiprivate rooms,* and *meal programs.* I couldn't breathe. This was for Hammy. They were going to send her away.

It all made sense now. Mom wasn't blind; she had seen things too. My knees started to wobble and I reached for an old stool we kept in the garage. I sat down and thought hard as I flipped through the pages of these glossy brochures. Hammy wasn't so bad that she needed this—she just needed a little help! The thought of her living in a seniors' home made me so sad. The pictures tried to make those places look so happy and cheery, but I wasn't fooled. How could you be happy living far away from the people who cared about you? What about Haji? How could he do without her? What would *I* do without her shuffling around her old house, passing me plates of nicely presented food after school? No. She was *not* going to the Golden Sunset Active Living Centre. Not yet. Not if I could do something, *anything* to help her.

Chapter 23

TREASURE HUNTING

Haji honked the car horn at ten o'clock. I was sitting in the living room waiting for him. "I'm leaving now! Haji's here!" I shouted to nobody in particular.

"Okay! Have fun!" Mom shouted back from the kitchen.

I opened the door to Haji's rental car and hopped in. Their car was still in the repair shop.

"I'm sorry this will be late, Peter. It's just so . . ." He struggled to finish his sentence.

"It's okay, Haji," I reassured him. I buckled my seat belt.

"Where can I take you?" he asked. "Metrotown? Haji not really know what to buy you. Hammy usually does all the shopping."

"Haji, do you know where Main Street is?"

"Main Street?" he said, confused. "No mall there."

"I don't want to go to the mall."

"Only thing on Main Street I know is Hammy's favorite old furniture stores," he replied, thinking hard.

"Exactly. Let's go." I stared straight ahead and he started to drive.

12:45 P.M.

It took all morning, but I found one. I didn't even care that it had a chipped ear.

"This is really all you want?" Haji asked. We were walking up Main Street to the big Chinese restaurant for dim sum. He opened the door for me and we walked up to the second floor.

I nodded. "Yes."

"But, Peter, you don't like pigs."

"Haji," I said, frustrated, "it's not for *me*."

He looked at me with his head tilted.

We sat down at a table for two in the corner. The waiter asked us something, but we looked up at him blankly. He switched to English. "Tea or water?"

"Tea for me, water for him," Haji replied.

I waited for a cart to pass by. That's the best thing about dim sum, the anticipation. The woman pushing a cart full of bamboo steamers headed toward us. I gestured for her to open the lids so I could see what was inside. I picked two of my favorite dishes. I don't know what they're called, the one with a big wad of diced shrimp and the one in a banana leaf full of sticky rice, but good food is yummy in any language.

Haji and I grabbed our chopsticks.

"Peter," Haji said after swallowing his first mouthful of rice. "I feel bad. Don't you want something else?"

I paused and thought about it. "Well, actually . . ."

"Tell me."

"I want you to take me to the hospital to see Hammy," I blurted out.

His mouth dropped. "Your mom not like that idea. She has very strong opinion. *Cha*, she's so bossy sometimes."

"She's not here, Haji," I said. "Don't you think I can handle it? I'm eleven now. She's my *grandmother*. I have a right to see her." I felt powerful.

"I don't know . . ."

"Haji, I know! I know everything. I saw Mom's brochures! If you're going to send Hammy away, I'd like to see her!" I was on the verge of yelling.

His shoulders sagged. "You know?"

"Yes, I know. But Mom doesn't know that I know, so let's keep it that way, okay?"

"Hammy not going for sure. Your mom just doing some research."

"It's a terrible idea!" I shouted.

"But Hammy not healthy anymore."

"She is too! She's still plenty healthy! She just has some bad days. We all have bad days, don't we?"

"Yes, sometimes my mind feels slow too. *Cha*, we all get old, I guess."

"So what's the rush?"

"I don't know." Haji looked deflated. "Your mom thinks it's best."

"Mom doesn't know everything."

Haji smirked. "You're right."

"Haji," I said super seriously. "What's going to happen to *you* if she goes into a home like that?"

He didn't say anything; he just stared at his plate. "Okay, I take you. After lunch. You need to see for yourself sooner or later."

Chapter 24

NEVER TELL ME THE ODDS

1:30 P.M.

CONDITIONS: STERILE

Haji stopped in his tracks and glanced over at me. "Peter, don't be nervous."

We were standing right outside Hammy's hospital room. My hands were damp and clammy. I started to feel my chest tighten up. I patted my pocket and hoped that by reassuring myself my inhaler was there, I wouldn't need it.

"Just relax." He put his hand over mine. I had been clutching the gift bag in my hand so hard my fingers had turned white.

The door was partially open, and Haji knocked lightly before he pushed it open wider. I followed him as he quietly walked into the room. Hammy's eyes were closed and she was sleeping. I watched her chest rise and fall gently and caught my own breath at the same time.

Hammy's skin was pale, almost gray. Her cheeks hollow. Her hair, which was usually so neat, was a mass of white wisps. I knew she had broken some bones, but seeing her left arm in a cast left me trembling. She looked so frail and weak.

"*Yobo*," Haji whispered in her ear. Her eyes opened slowly. She looked at Haji and smiled faintly.

Then she looked at me and said, "Ji Won." She forced herself to smile wider.

"Hi, Hammy." My mouth dried up and I couldn't think of anything else to say. I took a step toward her bed. I carefully put my hand over her right hand and felt her cool skin. I was surprised to see Trixie tucked under her arm in the cast, his head popping out from beneath her bent elbow.

"Peter has something for you," Haji offered, breaking the silence.

"I hope you like it." I nervously handed her the bag.

She smiled at me and her eyes wrinkled in the corners. Even in the hospital gown and with tubes coming out of her arms, her eyes still sparkled with warmth.

She used her good hand to reach into the bag and pull out the ceramic pig. My heart pounded furiously in my chest.

"What's this?" she asked as she held it in her hand and peered at it, turning it over a few times. I waited desperately for a smile, for a flicker of joy, something.

"A ceramic pig. They're your favorite," I said, trying to help her remember.

"Oh?" she answered.

She simply put the pig back in the bag.

"Thank you. I need water," Hammy said vaguely as my heart fell to the floor.

Haji gave me long look. His eyes were both kind and sad at the same time.

4:45 P.M.

After Haji dropped me off at home, I started to feel all sorts of weird stomach cramps. I walked directly into my room and closed the door. On my bed was a book with a bow on it. My belated birthday present from my parents: *Botany for the Budding Young Naturalist.* I threw the book in the corner and then myself on the floor and stared blankly at the ceiling.

Seeing Hammy like that was distressing. My mind, like my stomach, was doing flips. The only thing I wanted to do was to tell L.B., but I wasn't sure this was the right thing to do. I remembered that sometimes it's good to write everything down. What I needed was a list of pros and cons.

I grabbed a piece of paper, sat at my desk and drew a chart:

PROS — TELL L.B.	CONS — DON'T TELL L.B.
L.B. MISSES HAMMY	L.B. IS DRAMATIC AND FAINTS
L.B. DESERVES TO KNOW THE TRUTH	L.B. IS TOO YOUNG AND CAN'T HANDLE THE TRUTH
L.B. IS SMART AND CAN BE RATIONAL	L.B. IS TOO SMART AND WILL BE HYSTERICAL
L.B. COULD HELP ME FIGURE OUT A WAY TO KEEP HAMMY OUT OF A SENIORS' HOME	MOM WILL KILL ME

It was even, a draw, a stalemate. I couldn't think of any other good reasons to tell L.B. or to not tell L.B. I put my pencil down and stared at the ceiling again.

I knew I should have been thinking about Hammy, but for some reason my mind started to wander. The last time I had done this pros and cons exercise was for our social studies unit, and I had to listen to Ryan explain why, in 1871, British Columbia should have never joined Confederation. His stupid bangs flashed before my eyes. The sight of his smug face whispering to me about entering the Royal Tyrrell

Museum newsletter contest was like a video playing in a loop in my brain.

To turn off the bad video in my head, I pulled out a fresh sheet of paper. A very teensy-tiny part of me admitted that I couldn't let him just win like that. I'd hate myself. A significantly larger portion of me admitted that it was probably hopeless. I hadn't actually given the contest much thought lately. Well, actually, I had given the contest no thought at all. Suddenly, I felt like maybe, just maybe, I should give it a little thought. I tapped my pencil on the edge of my desk. I was hoping that inspiration would just strike and my hand would miraculously start drawing something amazing. Instead, L.B. opened my bedroom door.

I groaned. "Not now, L.B.!"

"What did Haji buy you?" she asked as she peeked in through the door. She didn't have that loud, sharp voice anymore. It seemed to have disappeared when Hammy went to the hospital.

"Nothing," I said flatly. I wasn't lying. He hadn't bought *me* anything.

"Nothing?"

"Okay, he bought me lunch," I answered.

"Did he tell you anything else?" I knew she was fishing for information about Hammy.

I took a quick breath through my nose and stared at my little sister. She was wearing leggings with small rainbows on them and a T-shirt covered in pink and purple ponies. Her hair had grown long, and she had put a single, uneven braid down the side of her face.

I glanced down at my list, and then I looked at her. Never mind my pros and cons list. L.B. needed to know.

"L.B.," I said, sitting up straight. "Come in and close the door. I have a lot to tell you."

Chapter 25

WANTED: MORE SPACE

Hammy was being released tomorrow. She had been in the hospital for thirteen days now, but it had felt a lot longer than that.

As I came into the kitchen for breakfast, I stepped over L.B. She was lying on the floor eating a piece of toast. Mom had given up trying to get her to sit at the table. Dad was already reading the newspaper. L.B. took the information I'd given her yesterday surprisingly well. While I was telling her, it had been obvious she needed something to hug, since Trixie was with Hammy, so I offered her my arm. It was still sore. I swore her to secrecy, because Mom could never find out that I had seen Hammy—that would have landed Haji in a hot mess of trouble with Mom and, for once, L.B. had kept her big mouth quiet.

I went to my usual spot at the table and waiting for me was *Astronomy for Stargazers*. I sighed and pushed the book to the middle of the table.

"Good morning, Peter." Mom frowned at me as she lifted up the book with two hands and moved it to the small desk in the kitchen.

"Hi." I yawned while I rubbed my head to try to wake up.

She placed an empty bowl in front of me and gestured for me to help myself to breakfast.

I was pushing some cereal around my bowl when Mom said, "I have something to tell you. Well, half-ask, half-tell."

I looked up. L.B. even turned her head to listen. "What do you mean?" I asked.

"So . . . ," she said cautiously. "Your dad and I were thinking—"

"Don't bring me into this!" he declared, looking up from his newspaper.

"Okay, *I* was thinking that it might be nice for Hammy and Haji to live here for a little while, just so we can keep a close eye on Hammy and make sure she's okay."

L.B., crumbs on her face, bolted up into a sitting position. She dropped her toast on the floor. "That's a splendid idea."

Mom got a broom and started sweeping crumbs. "But, as you know, we don't have an extra room."

"Our sofa is very comfortable," L.B. said. "I have spent many hours on it this week."

"Yes, I know." Mom sighed, staring at her sideways as she dumped the crumbs into the compost. "But it's not really a good idea to have Hammy and Haji sleep on the same sofa, is it?" She looked at us silently. "So . . . we're—"

Dad cut her off. "You mean, *you're!*"

"Okay, okay, *I'm* thinking that . . ." She was talking so slowly it was weird. Then she just suddenly blurted out, "Starting tomorrow, you two will share a room, and Hammy and Haji will take the other person's room, okay?" She said that whole sentence in about two seconds.

"What?" I declared. "Did I hear that right?"

L.B. perked up and said happily, "Today just keeps getting better and better!"

I slapped my hand to my forehead. I knew it was for the best. Hammy was well enough to be released from the hospital and that was a good thing. That was an amazing thing. But memories of sharing a hotel room during our road trip flooded over me.

I went to my room, closed the door and tried to enjoy the feeling of quiet solitude, because tomorrow, L.B. was moving in. This wasn't going to be fun at all.

Chapter 26

RESISTANCE IS FUTILE

"It's temporary," Mom said as she and Dad carried my mattress out of my room.

"It had better be!" I muttered through clenched teeth.

They moved my bed into L.B.'s room so that Hammy and Haji could sleep on our beds pushed together. L.B. and I were going to be sleeping on foam mattresses on the floor of my room.

Haji arrived with a suitcase full of stuff for their stay.

"Her scarf! Did you pack her scarf?" Mom said as she rummaged around the suitcase.

"I packed four scarves! I know her favorites."

"Her cardigans! Where are her cardigans?"

209

"*Cha*, relax! If she needs something, we can always go back to the house to get it," Haji said softly.

Mom sat down on the edge of my bed, which was now crammed against the wall in L.B.'s room.

She rubbed her eyes. "You're right."

Haji sat and put his arm around her. "You have done good job. Hammy will be comfortable."

Mom smiled at him, but it didn't hide that she looked a bit sad.

10:15 A.M.

CONDITIONS: NERVOUS WRECK. CAN'T EVEN LOOK OUTSIDE

Dad stayed home while we waited for Mom and Haji to bring Hammy back. I was nervous for L.B. I mean, I had told her how banged up Hammy looked and how Hammy seemed more forgetful than ever, but hearing about something and actually seeing it are two totally different things.

L.B. sat outside the front door the minute Mom and Haji pulled away.

"They won't be back for at least an hour," Dad said, trying to get her to come inside.

"Then I'll wait here for at least one hour," she replied simply.

Her hands were empty because she didn't have Trixie anymore, so instead she restlessly wrapped a piece of string around her finger over and over until her fingertip turned blue. Then she would release the string, allow blood to return to her finger and tie the string around again.

Dad stood in the doorway watching her. "L.B., how about you make Hammy a nice picture? Like a welcome-home banner or something like that."

She turned to face him. "Will she even notice?"

I walked quickly to the door. "That's a great idea, Dad. Come on, L.B. We'll make her something nice." I put out my hand for her.

She slowly stood and took my hand. "Okay, Petey, let's make her a sign." I grabbed the piece of string out of her hand and shoved it in my pocket.

I told L.B. to cut pieces of colored paper into strips and make a paper chain. While she was gluing, I found the largest piece of paper we had and I drew big block letters that said "Welcome Home!"

"Why don't you glue your chain around the outside of the paper, like a nice border?" I said to her.

She looked at me pitifully. "I know what you're doing."

"I'm making a sign."

"You're keeping me busy."

"Just start gluing. When you're done, color in these letters."

"This is busy work. My teachers use this strategy on me regularly. It's hardly original."

"If it's good enough for them, it's good enough for me."

She sighed.

"It's better than you amputating your own finger, right? Glue!" I instructed.

"After we're done, can we go back to the front door?" she asked. I nodded.

She squeezed a huge dollop of glue onto the paper and, without any regard for straight lines or visual appeal, she slapped the chain down and glue oozed everywhere. I stared at the glob of glue and the haphazardly constructed chain. It took everything I had to not adjust her work. The girl had no flair for presentation.

L.B. was coloring outside the lines with a red marker when we heard the van door close. We both stopped what we were doing and immediately stood up.

"Come on," I said. We went to the front. L.B. suddenly bolted back inside and she prowled around the kitchen table. It was like she didn't know what to do with herself, so she just kept walking in a circle.

I ran back to the table to get the half-finished sign.

"Don't you want to hold the sign?" I asked L.B.

She shook her head and continued to pace.

Mom had already exited the van and was on the passenger side helping Hammy. Gingerly, Hammy put one foot down on the pavement and slowly the next. I could see that she was wearing her favorite yellow cardigan, but it was draped over her shoulders because, with her cast, she couldn't put her arm through the sleeve. With some effort and Mom's help, Hammy finally pushed herself off the seat.

Haji and Mom flanked Hammy, helping her come into the house.

"Hi, Hammy." I smiled as I stepped aside to let her in the door. I held my tension as far away from me as I could and pretended to be cool. "Welcome home!" I lifted the sign a little bit.

"Hello." She reached over with her good hand and gave my cheek a light pat. "Beautiful sign, thank you. Where's L.B.?" Hammy's eyes scanned the living room.

With her good arm, Hammy reached into her purse and pulled out Trixie. She tucked him under her arm, just like L.B. used to hold him.

L.B. had crept out of the kitchen, but instead of greeting Hammy, she practically hid behind me.

Hammy's eyes lit up. "L.B. Why so shy? It's me!"

L.B. stayed behind me and said, "Hi, Hammy." She stared at the ground before she ventured to say, "Are you okay?"

"Hammy's arm a little bit . . . hurt." She gestured to her cast. "But not bad for old lady!"

L.B. emerged from behind me.

"I think you probably want him back now." Hammy leaned over stiffly, holding Trixie out for L.B. "When I was lonely, I hold him, and I think of you. He helped me so much, thank you."

L.B. held Hammy's gaze. Her hand reached out, tentatively at first, but then suddenly grabbed Trixie and in the same motion reached out and grasped Hammy's waist.

"I knew it! I knew he would make you feel better!" She buried him in her face and inhaled deeply.

"We stay here for a little while, until Hammy's arm gets better, and then when I go home, I make you special Korean food. You probably not had good Korean food lately." Hammy stared at my mom.

Mom looked irritated and pursed her lips together. Dad put his arm around her.

"Let me show you your room!" L.B. smiled shyly as she took Hammy's hand and led her upstairs.

Haji stood by the front door and watched Hammy and L.B. go upstairs slowly. I gave him a crooked smile, which he returned.

8:30 P.M., TIME TO MEET MY MAKER
CONDITIONS: PARADISE LOST (ALSO A BIT OVERCAST)

Within just twelve hours, my room, which had always been my sanctuary, my own private escape, was now filled with the oppressive excitability and enthusiasm of L.B. There was a surreal, horror-movie element to my life now, because I was sleeping on a thin piece of foam with my sister's face only two feet away from me.

When we were settling in, she let out an ear-piercing shriek, followed by a series of exploding giggles. She was back to her old, unbearable self.

"Quit it!" I said to her angrily.

"Sorry," she said, smirking. "This is just so incredible! It has been a thrilling day. Hammy's return, and now this!" Then she got all serious and tried hard to stop smiling. "I promise to give Petey some space."

I looked at her skeptically.

"But when in REM sleep, it's impossible to predict what may happen!"

Hammy and Haji poked their heads into the room.

"Good night," they said.

"Like camping!" Haji said, laughing.

"Good night," I muttered. I did *not* think it was funny at all.

"Good night, everyone!" L.B. chirped happily as Hammy and Haji closed the door.

L.B. settled into her area with a very satisfied look on her face. She pulled the sheet up under her chin and then started giggling again.

"L.B., *please* . . . ," I begged.

"In many parts of the world, it's common for large families to all sleep together in the same room, often even the same bed." She wasn't fooling me one bit.

"Well, this is *Canada*! We don't have to live like that, do we?" I asked indignantly. She opened her mouth to reply, but I interrupted her. "That was a *rhetorical* question! Don't say another word!" I pointed my finger at her as she tried to resume a straight face, and I flipped over onto my side so my back was turned to her. I fitfully went to sleep.

When I woke up, L.B.'s arms and legs were completely draped over me. She was a mouth breather. She breathed in and then blew her toxic breath out—directly into my face.

I pushed her off of me.

She took a few seconds to wake up and said, "Petey, what is it?"

"You have absolutely the worst breath in the world!" I yelled as I fanned my face.

"Halitosis is common in the morning!" L.B. pouted.

I stomped across the hallway and tried to get into the bathroom, but the door was locked.

"It's Haji! Almost done!" Then I heard the toilet flush.

I waited outside the door for Haji to emerge.

"Good morning, Peter!" Haji said happily. He tucked a Korean newspaper under his arm and moved aside to let me in.

I walked into the washroom and immediately gagged. How much could one person tolerate? I mean, I was grateful Hammy had been released from the hospital, I really was. I would be even more grateful if Haji would start using Mom and Dad's washroom instead.

Chapter 27

A RISKY CHOICE

With everything that had happened with my family this summer, I'd hardly seen Joe at all. He texted me and we decided to meet up this afternoon to hang out. I hadn't told him too much about our trip; in fact, the only word I used to describe it to him when he'd asked was *fine*, but that was the opposite of the truth.

We walked to the 7-Eleven on the corner of Kingsway and Joyce Street and poured ourselves extra-large Slurpees. The choice of flavor for the base layer was key to mixing a quality Slurpee. Today was a Coca-Cola kind of day. I topped it with a thick layer of Orange Crush.

"I'm going to try the spicy mango," Joe said, smiling mischievously and pulling at the lever.

"You're going to regret it," I warned him.

"Sometimes you just gotta take a risk, you know?"

I shrugged. I guess he was right, but sometimes it was also good to play it safe.

After we paid for our drinks, we decided to walk by Gaston Park. We weren't going to play soccer or anything, we had both worn sandals, but hoped there might be something interesting going on. Hanging out with Joe again felt good. It was like things were getting back to normal.

"Whoa!" Joe yelped in surprise after his first long sip.

"Told you."

"No, no. It's actually pretty good!" He resumed sucking on his straw. "Seriously. Try it." He held his cup out for me.

I shook my head no. Firstly, sharing straws—yuck. Secondly, I was happy with my normal flavors.

Even if the weather is beautiful, the last weekend before school always has this dark cloud hanging over it. I know what's coming in just a few short days and there's nothing I can do to stop it. Specifically, Ryan. I'd already seen that punk once this summer, and soon I'd have to see him all the time. I wasn't emotionally prepared.

At the park, there was a group of old women doing tai chi, and even though I couldn't understand what they were saying, there was still something so familiar in their faces and I was reminded of Hammy.

"Wanna go sit on the swings?" Joe asked.

I shrugged. "Sure."

We both planted our bottoms into seats and, using our toes, we gently rocked ourselves, twisting our bodies but never going very high because it was hard to hold a Slurpee cup and do some serious swinging.

The playground was one of the newer kinds, with a bouncy rubber floor, brightly colored slides and a small arrangement of bars to climb over and through. Next to the swings, there was a big pit of sand. On a small hill next to the sand, a water feature, like a small metal channel, where you could control the stream of water with movable dams. If you manually kept pumping the water and didn't block it with the dams, the stream eventually flooded part of the sand, turning it into a mud pit. There were a few kids with shovels and buckets, digging and laughing. They were kicking up a lot of dust. I watched them while drinking.

"Fools." I thought that I had said that word only in my head, but apparently I hadn't.

"Who's the fool?" Joe asked.

"Those kids." I gestured over to the innocent faces. "I hope none of them has asthma."

Joe looked confused.

"Asthma and dust. It's a bad combination, believe me."

I sucked up the rest of my drink but, like summer, it hadn't lasted long enough.

Chapter 28

A WET BLANKET

My school always starts the year in a weird way. We go to school for one hour. One measly hour. It's mostly just to take attendance, but what it really does is leave you feeling in limbo. I had to go back to Mr. Costa's classroom and sit at my old desk. Even though I knew I was in sixth grade now, it still *felt* like fifth grade.

Ryan showed up on the first day of school wearing a Kukkiwon Taekwondo shirt. Was he trolling me? Something about it grated on my nerves. Like now he was even stealing my cultural stuff, which he had no business stealing. Looking at him made me simmer like hot soup in a stone bowl.

I heard him say to Liam, "My parents found me the best taekwondo class in the city. My master went out to

222

dinner with the head coach of the Kukkiwon team when they were in town and they invited my class to Seoul next summer!"

I didn't think it was possible, but my rage increased.

When we were finally assigned our new classes, Ryan was in my class—again. Obviously, I was cursed. I almost wanted to ask L.B. what the statistical odds of that happening were, but at the same time, I didn't want to know. There were always two classes for each grade, but somehow Ryan and I always ended up in the same one. After seven years with this guy (including kindergarten!), I needed a break. I even got Stephanie Aquino too.

"Sorry, man," Joe said to me as my fate became obvious.

"Lucky you," I said to him as he went off to the *other* sixth-grade class.

The usual group quickly restarted our daily soccer games. It was just natural for us to all run to the field, but from the very first day back, my head wasn't ever really in the game. Ryan wasted no time resuming his "king of the pitch" attitude. He tried to score on me from anywhere and everywhere. He didn't let the other players have a turn. He got furious when he was open and nobody passed to him. He was angry if he got checked. He gloated like an inflated peacock when he scored.

Soccer wasn't fun anymore. I could feel our game breaking up.

Joe came up to me during a pause in the game yesterday and said, "I know it's only the first week back, but is it just me or is he worse this year?"

"You think so too?" I asked, relieved that it wasn't all in my head.

"Yeah, something about him this year. He's driving me crazy. Like he's making me hate soccer," Joe confessed as he wiped his forehead with the back of his hand. "I'm thinking of hanging somewhere else. I'm sick of this." He'd pointed with his index finger in the general area of Ryan.

I didn't think he was any different from last year, not really, but this year, he felt *unbearable*. Maybe the rest of us had changed. A few boys just stopped showing up to the field and instead trickled away to the basketball court. I eyed the seventh-grade boys laughing and having a good time.

"In your face, Peter!" Ryan shouted now as he ran by doing his victory lap. It was the fourth time he had scored on me that day. I felt as though the net got bigger over the summer and somehow I got smaller. Every single ball seemed to get past me. And since Joe was true to his word and hadn't showed up at the soccer field today, choosing to hang out near the basketball court instead, I felt worse.

I threw off my gloves. "I'm out!" I yelled.

"Peter!" Liam shouted at me as he jogged my way. "You can't quit! Nobody else wants to play goalie. We're already so short on players!"

"I'm not feeling great today," I lied. I felt okay. I put my hand to my chest for dramatic effect.

"Just scared of being scored on for the millionth time this week, *Petey?*" Ryan said mockingly.

Something in me finally broke. I couldn't keep quiet. "Stuff it, *elf*," I replied.

"What did you say?" Ryan asked in disbelief.

"You heard me," I replied calmly. I took a confident step forward, towering over him, and even though my guts were quaking inside, I tried not to show it. I saw something in Ryan's eyes that I had never seen before. Instead of holding my gaze, he turned away.

"You don't have to be such a bully!" Ryan said, sounding surprised.

Ryan really was unbelievable—he could dish it out, but he sure couldn't take it when the tables were turned.

The bell rang, and it gave everybody an excuse to retreat. Ryan scowled at me and sprinted toward the school, but I walked calmly with a smile erupting on my face.

CONDITIONS: FROSTY

My sixth-grade teacher, Ms. Tran, told us she was going to assign us big projects this year. She was one of those teachers who never yelled and she smelled like cupcakes. She wore thick cardigans to match her thick glasses. We were in the library working on our new science unit, which I normally would have loved, but today I felt no excitement about it. I felt sorry for Ms. Tran when I saw that Ryan had trapped her into a one-sided conversation about himself. He wasn't trying to keep his voice down at all.

"My mother compiled a list of all these writing contests she says I should enter." He showed Ms. Tran a sheet of paper full of information.

"Wow, I didn't know there were so many writing competitions available for kids!"

"Well, as you know, Ms. Tran, my mother is an award-winning journalist. Did you see her recent piece on corruption in the oil and gas industry?"

She shook her head no.

"I'm surprised. You really should be more up-to-date on your current affairs." He looked at her with disbelief. "Anyway, she keeps track of all these things for me. There

226

are a few I'm especially interested in." He was speaking more loudly than before. "The Royal Tyrrell Museum, for instance, has an open call for submissions. They announced it in a newsletter in June, but I have another few weeks before the deadline."

I glanced up. He was staring right at me.

"I'm going to write an excellent piece on what it takes to be a *paleontologist*." He didn't take his eyes off me. "I expect it will be prominently featured when I *win*."

"I didn't know that you had an interest in paleontology, Ryan," Ms. Tran said.

"Oh, no, I don't," Ryan said, looking disgusted. "What a joke. I'm just writing it to win. Pad my résumé, as my mom says."

"Well, good luck on those, Ryan," Ms. Tran said, trying to make her escape.

"I don't need luck, Ms. Tran. I've got talent."

I took a long, slow breath. I tried very hard not to care. I wasn't going to be a paleontologist anyway, but *he* didn't know how badly my summer had gone. Still, the mention of the museum stabbed me where it hurt. I refused to give him the satisfaction and I held my expression as emotionless as possible.

But at home, I went on a rampage.

"Mom!" I shouted. "I need garbage bags and boxes!"

"Why?" she asked as she poked her head into my room.

"It's time to get rid of stuff!"

"What's the sudden urge to clean your room?" She was holding something behind her back.

"It's time. All these dinosaur things, they've all got to go."

"You've really given up the idea of being a paleontologist?" she asked, slouching her shoulders and unable to hide her disappointment.

I stared at her in disbelief. "Yes, Mom!" I said impatiently. "Were you not there this summer? Did you not see what happened?"

She looked at me, unimpressed. "Yes, I was there, Peter. I'm sorry we weren't more cautious before the dig. But you can manage your asthma—it shouldn't manage you. I don't think one small setback should stop you from fulfilling a lifelong dream. It was wonderful that you had an ambition, especially because it was scientific. But now you don't seem to have one . . . ," she said, looking vaguely around my room. She stared at the shelves in Dino Grotto, where my paleontology books and dinosaur figures stood neat and orderly, now covered with a fine layer of dust.

"Seriously, Mom? Give me a break!" I exclaimed. Struggling for air on a sunbaked rock was hardly a small setback!

"Okay, then, how about molecular biology?" she suggested. "Has that very good microscope sparked anything yet? You've got all those really great slides. Haji spent a lot of money on it."

"No!" I shouted, feeling pained and frustrated. "You can't just *hope* I'm going to love a new branch of science, Mom! You can't force molecular biology or astronomy or botany on me. It's just got to happen on its own. Believe me, it hasn't happened yet!" Dinosaurs had ripped out my heart; how could I just quickly move on to something else?

"Well, clearly you are not in a reasonable mood to discuss your future," she said stiffly. No, I wasn't. "I guess I'll just see if I can get my money back for this." From behind her back emerged a book, *Through the Microscope: A Primer for Biologists.* "But, it is something you need to think about—when you're ready," she said as she turned to leave my room. She adjusted the book awkwardly in her arms as she tried to get a free hand to smooth down the ends of her hair. "This discussion isn't over. Bags or boxes?"

"Both." I quietly fumed while I waited for her to return.

Mom came back with several boxes and a few large garbage bags. She silently placed them on my floor and left.

I zeroed in on Dino Grotto. I was going to have to stop calling it that. I started pulling dinosaur books off my shelves and threw them into boxes. Because my parents will spend any amount of money on an educational book, I had every dinosaur book I had ever wanted or needed. My shelves were completely full, but not for long.

I filled up all the boxes Mom had given me within minutes. I continued my mass dinosaur extermination. Next, dinosaur figurines. Three more garbage bags of those. The sharp claws kept ripping the plastic and the figurines kept falling out. It was almost as if they were refusing to be bagged up.

I finally cleaned off my shelves and stared at the bags and boxes on the floor. I just wanted to get all this stuff out of my sight, I just couldn't look at it anymore, so I opened my closet doors. My field vest stared right at me. I needed to get rid of that too. As I ripped it off the hanger, my old *Field Notes and Observations* journal and some tools fell out of the vest. I shoved the vest and the tools into a bag, but I picked up the journal.

It should have felt familiar, but the weight of it in my hands felt strange. I turned it over a few times before I opened it. I flipped through the pages I had so carefully and meticulously drawn in over the years. I could not believe that I had wasted so much of my life making this book. All the notes, all the observations and those photocopied grids. Everything was so neat, so tidy. My face started to feel flushed and I felt a tightening in my chest. It was like my body's cruel little reminder of who was really in charge. I tried to focus and to just breathe, but I gave up and reached into my pocket for my inhaler.

I threw my journal on top of a box, and then I pushed all the boxes and all the bags into the back of my closet, as deep as they would go. It all reminded me that I was an idiot and Ryan was already doing a good job of that.

Chapter 29

THE VERY DEFINITION OF COLIC

L.B. was curled up in Hammy's lap, hugging Trixie. Hammy was stroking L.B.'s hair and twisting it and then letting it go. I stopped halfway down the stairs to watch them. They did a lot of this lately, just sitting together. Sometimes talking, sometimes just watching TV, sometimes L.B. staying with Hammy even if Hammy was taking a nap. I felt like I was intruding a little bit, listening like this, but I also didn't want to interrupt them.

"Tell me the story again!" L.B. said impatiently.

"Which story?"

"The story about how you saved everyone's sanity when I was a baby."

Hammy laughed. "Oh, that's a good story."

L.B. turned so she was staring straight up at Hammy.

Hammy cleared her throat and began. "When you came back from hospital, you were so tiny, but so loud. Crying all the time. Nonstop crying."

L.B. chuckled.

"I remember your mom was *so* tired because no matter what she did, you wouldn't stop crying. She carried you, you cried. She put you in stroller, you cried. She took you for a drive, you cried. She was going crazy."

"That's because I had colic!"

"Peter asked your dad, 'What's colic?' and your dad say, holding you far away from him, '*This* is colic!'" Hammy laughed. She did a great impersonation of Dad.

"Of course we now know that colic is abdominal pain, likely caused by excess gas in the intestines."

I almost burst out laughing. L.B. *was* a natural-born gasbag, wasn't she?

"But when I came to hold you, you always stopped crying. Sometimes not right away, but usually I tell you stories or sing you a song quietly in your ear. Then it's like you stopped crying just to listen."

L.B. smiled. "I *was* listening. I'm always listening."

"You very good girl." Hammy stroked L.B.'s hair again. "Hammy always know that."

Suddenly, a series of pictures flashed across my mind. Hammy playing hide-and-go-seek with us. Hammy walking me home from school. Hammy making me noodles. Hammy laughing and giving L.B. piggybacks. Hammy sleeping on the floor next to L.B.'s crib so L.B. would sleep.

I watched the two of them together and realized that the old Hammy—she was still there. She was worth fighting for. L.B. needed her. *I* needed her.

Quietly, I sprinted upstairs to my room and closed the door behind me. Something made my breathing ragged and halting. I patted my right pocket for my inhaler. Before I knew what I was doing, I reached for my left pocket, but stopped myself short. My hand balled into a fist. I knew what I needed to do, but I took a minute to compose myself. I wasn't sure I was ready. But I had to do it. It was for Hammy. I walked to my desk, opened the drawer and pulled out a fresh coil notebook. There were a lot of ideas swirling around my head and they needed to be organized. This was the only way.

9:30 P.M.

CONDITIONS: INSOMNIA

I held my blanket tight up around my chin. Sleeping seemed impossible with so much on my mind.

"L.B.," I whispered. No response. "L.B.!" I raised my voice slightly.

"Hmm?" she responded sleepily.

"Oh good, you're awake." I sat up and shook her shoulders. "We have to talk."

Her eyes popped open. "I am fully awake and ready to engage!" She sat up too.

"I've been doing some research." I reached under my foam mattress for some pages I had printed off the Internet. I placed my coil notebook on the top of the pile.

"Me too!" She reached under her mattress and pulled out an even thicker stack of pages.

She couldn't let me just have the bigger pile of paper, could she?

"We need a plan."

"I agree completely, Petey."

"Tell me what you've been reading about."

A huge smile erupted on her face.

"Please don't start giggling—it's late."

She took a deep breath and said, "You're right. I'll try to be calm." Still, she continued to smile like a fool. "But you understand how exciting this is for me, don't you?"

I sighed. "L.B., we're just talking."

"Exactly. Brother to sister. Sister to brother. Equals in a scheme of great importance."

"Why can't you just talk like a normal human being?"

"That wouldn't be true to my character."

"Okay, whatever. Let's just figure out something. Hammy is *not* going to any place like the Golden Sunset Active Living Centre."

"Agreed," L.B. said solemnly.

Chapter 30

HE SHOOTS! HE SCORES!

MONDAY, SEPTEMBER 9, AFTER LUNCH
CONDITIONS: BREEZY, AND WITH A CHANCE OF
LANDING A THREE-POINTER

I talked to Samuel today for the first time since August. He had dyed his hair with blond streaks and had started to wear an earring. I don't know too much about jewelry, but it sure looked like a real diamond. His clothes looked different too. He still played basketball, but he didn't look sporty anymore; he had crossed the line into athleisure wear—those fancy clothes that *look* like they're for sports, but you're not supposed to actually exercise in them. I heard the seventh-grade girls gossiping about him going back to Korea to try out for a boy band next summer. The girls thought it was the coolest thing ever. It made sense. He looked perfect for the part.

I know for a fact that Samuel's Korean name is Sung Ho because that's what his grandmother calls him. I guess that's a good name for a boy who wants to be in a K-pop group.

"What did you do to Ryan?" he asked me. Standing right next to him in the middle of the hallway made me feel more uncool than usual.

"What?" I asked, surprised that he would know or care.

"Ryan. He hates your guts," Samuel said.

"Well, I don't like him very much either." I paused. "Also, I might have called him an elf."

"Ha, that's funny." Samuel laughed. "Just givin' you a heads-up, bro, that boy ain't nice." Who didn't know *that*? "You know he plays up a division in soccer now, so we're on the same team, right?"

I nodded. Of course I knew Ryan played in a league with older boys; he wouldn't let anybody forget. Nobody questioned Ryan's soccer skills—just his personality.

"During soccer practice, he was talkin' trash, like he was entering some museum writing contest just to flaunt it in your face." He stopped to look at me. "I don't know how that dude thinks a writing contest is cool, but whatever." Samuel shrugged his shoulders.

"Oh, thanks, Samuel. That's good to know." Ryan had gone too far. Bragging to Samuel during soccer practice about beating *me*?

"K-brothers for life." He flashed me a finger sign. I guess it kind of looked like a *K*.

I tried flashing it back to him, but I'm pretty sure I ended up giving him the finger. I was about to start walking away, but he looked like he wanted to keep talking.

"Hey, did you grow over the summer?" he asked, changing the subject.

I was taller than he was by at least a full head.

I shrugged my shoulders.

"Do you sing or dance?" he asked.

I shook my head.

"How about basketball?"

I shook my head again.

"Come on, man. *You* don't play basketball?" He eyed me up and down. Why did everybody assume I played basketball?

"Being a soccer goalie has always been my thing. Until recently," I said. "Plus, I have asthma. Sometimes a lot of running isn't great for me."

"So what? I have asthma too."

"You do?" I said, surprised.

"Yeah, it's getting better every year. Just got to be careful about your triggers. I mean, everybody's different, but I never want to let asthma stop me from doing what I want. Neither should you."

The bell rang and I was going to be late for class, but I couldn't pull myself away. I just found myself staring at Samuel with my head tilted.

"Come shoot some hoops after school. Joe's already joined us. No pressure, just fun."

I straightened my back. "Can't today. My mom wants me to stay home with my sister when her math tutor comes over," I explained. Haji had to take Hammy to a lot of appointments these days, so some days we have to walk home without them. I hoped this situation was temporary.

"Yeah, your sister," he said vaguely. "Okay, tomorrow at lunch. No excuses, dude."

I tried to keep cool, but I couldn't close my jaw. Samuel had asked me to join the seventh-grade boys at basketball.

As Samuel walked away, he turned around and said loudly, "I hope your *halmoni* is doing okay."

TUESDAY, SEPTEMBER 10, LUNCH
CONDITIONS: CALM-ISH

The next day, after I took my morning puff, I put on my best track pants and nicest athletic T-shirt. At lunch I could see the boys were trying to get a soccer game together, but still nobody had volunteered to be goalie. I realized that maybe I had been the only sucker who had willingly played that position all these years, and my ears felt warm.

I walked over to the courts and spied Samuel.

"Peter!" he called out to me. I jogged over and felt the comforting slap of my inhaler in my pocket.

"Oh, this kid!" one of his friends said, laughing. "He's on *my* team!"

"Samuel." I pulled him aside. "I'm warning you, I'm not very good at basketball."

"Dude, just stand under the net. When somebody comes along, jump and swat the ball away. No problem," he said as he looked at me reassuringly.

"Let's play!" one of the boys shouted.

They started with a jump ball and Samuel got control of the ball first. He dribbled up the court and deked left, leaving Joe, who was trying to guard him, standing like a statue. Samuel ran under the net and did a graceful layup. The ball hit the backboard and then dropped straight through the hoop. The game transitioned quickly and offensive players soon switched to their defensive roles.

"Peter!" Samuel shouted. "He's coming!" He pointed to another boy, so I carefully watched him come down the court.

He was going for a jump shot, so I timed it and swatted the ball away.

"Nice block!" the boys said, and several offered me a high five.

That feeling of smacking the basketball away was more like soccer than I realized. But better because Ryan wasn't here. Just for a little while, as I dribbled, passed and blocked, I forgot that Ryan was probably going to get the lead story in the Royal Tyrrell newsletter, and while I was laughing, I didn't think about how much that was going to destroy me.

Chapter 31

LAST GASP

THURSDAY, SEPTEMBER 12, 6:20 P.M.

CONDITIONS: HIGH-PRESSURE RIDGE HOLDING

"Petey!" L.B. said, rushing into my room with tears in her eyes.

"What's wrong?" I closed my coil notebook.

"I can't do it!" L.B. threw herself down on the ground next to my foam mattress, and bits of paper went everywhere.

"Do what?" I asked wearily. I wasn't in the mood for her theatrics right now.

"You know the thing we talked about?" she said secretively.

"Yes, it *was* my idea."

"I have been doing more research as you suggested. Look at this article!" She thrust a page printed off from the computer in my face, and she had circled a section of it in red marker: "Support at Home for Dementia Patients: Practical Tips for Creating Safe Spaces."

I quietly read the article and looked at the illustrations.

"This is actually a good idea," I said. "So why are you upset?"

"I really want to help Hammy. But I *can't do it!*" she wailed as she writhed on the floor. "And we're running out of time! I heard Mom and Dad whispering about an appointment at a new seniors' home in Surrey. They serve Korean food! They said it sounded perfect for Hammy. Do you know how far Surrey is? On a map, it is only a twenty-minute drive, but when you account for the severe traffic conditions we increasingly are seeing in this area, that means it's too far to see her regularly! This will not do!"

"Come on," I said as I pulled her up so she was sitting on the floor. "You *are* helping Hammy."

"How am I helping? I can't do *this!*" She pointed at the article. "My printing is *terrible!* My drawings are *worse!*" she cried as she violently shredded up sheets of paper. "You have to do it. You have to help Hammy! We cannot let Mom and Dad move her so far away!"

She finally remembered to breathe, then she continued, "It's like what you used to do, remember?" She looked directly at my closet, where I had put all my dinosaur stuff.

She jumped up, threw open the door and immediately started to paw through my boxes.

"L.B.!" I bellowed. "Get out of there! That's private!"

As fast as an annoying housefly, she found what she was looking for. "Here!" She showed me page sixty-seven from *Fossil Dreams: A Young Scientist's Essential Guide*, then she compared it to the article she had printed. "Do you see, Petey? There are clear parallels!"

She looked at me pleadingly.

I glanced at my book and back to the sheet of paper. My eyes opened wide and I met L.B.'s gaze.

"I know you can do it, Petey."

L.B. was right: between the two of us, I was the only one with the skills to get this done. I knew *exactly* what I needed to do and how to do it. Our vague plan finally had a clear direction.

Chapter 32

WHAT'S THAT SMELL?

FRIDAY, SEPTEMBER 13, 8:50 P.M.

CONDITIONS: PATIENTLY WAITING FOR BAD LUCK

TO STRIKE

I sat at my desk in my room and I smelled something bad. I looked around my desk for the source of the aroma that was a cross between a rotting Jamaican patty and an overripe apple. When I reached down to open the bottom drawer, I realized something. It was *me*. I was the cause of the offending stink. Mom was going to have to start buying me some deodorant. I guess I was going through the "change" we'd discussed in health and career development class. I had been playing basketball with the older boys for a few days now, and today I'd played longer and harder than ever before. The fact that I could smell myself was proof.

I looked forward to playing because, when I was on the court, it helped me forget about everything else. Today's bonus was Samuel's mom came to the court and brought Korean rice cakes for a snack. We hadn't had much Korean food since Hammy's accident, so my mouth started to drool when I saw what she was carrying.

His mom gave me a little wave. "How's your *halmoni?*" she asked.

"Okay," I answered. "She's staying with us until she gets better. Her cast is supposed to come off soon."

"Good news," she replied warmly as she handed Samuel the trays of rice cakes.

Then she spoke quickly to Samuel in Korean. He looked uncomfortable and embarrassed but took the food anyway. It was nice to see that even cool kids let their parents humiliate them.

We sat down on a bench to eat right away, because everybody knows Korean rice cakes taste good only the day they are made. Once you open the package, you have to eat it all or they get all hard and gross.

"What's that stuff?" Samuel's friend Jay Zhang asked. "Looks weird."

"Did I offer any to you?" Samuel shot back. "You think some of that Chinese stuff ain't weird? I have two words for you, Jay: *chicken feet.* You Chinese dudes got no business dissing Korean food!"

"Hey, they taste good!" Jay said.

"To *you*, bro," Samuel replied.

Jay rolled his eyes and continued to shoot baskets.

"At least *you* can appreciate these," he said to me as he passed me a Styrofoam tray.

I picked up a piece, laughing. "Well, even I don't like this one with bean very much." I picked out the dried beans embedded into the sticky rice cake.

"That's my favorite!" he said. "Don't waste the beans, man—eat the plain ones." He passed me the other tray.

There was a pause as we chewed.

"Hey, I heard a rumor. Are you planning on going back to Korea after this school year?" I asked.

"Probably."

"Oh."

"Gotta do what I was born to do, you know," he said. "Gotta try anyway. Otherwise, I'd always wonder. A life with regret ain't a good life." We finished our rice cakes and he slapped my leg to get me up and playing for a bit longer.

I was getting better at my jump shots. If there weren't too many guys around, Samuel did drills with me so I could get better. He was a good teacher. As long as I planned ahead and took a puff before the game, I never had to think about my lungs. Every time I took a jump shot, I felt my inhaler bounce in my pocket against my thigh. A little reminder that it was still there. And maybe it would always be there, but that was okay; it wasn't going to stop me from trying to shoot at least 50 percent from the field.

11:45 P.M.

After I'd washed the reek off of me, I crawled into bed and kept thinking about two things: Joe taking a risk and trying a spicy mango Slurpee and what Samuel said about living a life with regret. Their words played over and over in my mind. There was just something about my talk with Samuel today that got me thinking, something I had tried so hard not to think about. Whenever I closed my eyes, all I could see was the back page of the Royal Tyrrell Museum's newsletter. I stayed awake for a long time trying to ignore the itchy feeling in my hand. But L.B. was sound asleep, I didn't fight it anymore, and instead of closing my eyes, I pulled out a flashlight, some paper and a pencil, and I got to work.

The first thing I drew was a Cretaceous jungle scene. Lush and full of life. This was the period when flowering plants started to emerge. It was the time of rising sea levels and the age of the terrestrial dinosaurs most well-known to the general population, not paleontology-obsessed kids. I sketched and then looked hard at what I had drawn— the Titanosaurus roaming around foliage was *boring*, no action. I tossed the paper aside. The Mosasaurus popped into my mind, not a dinosaur but an ancient marine reptile; these were minor details the average person didn't care about. I froze. I couldn't remember if its fins had four or five digits.

All the dinosaur facts I used to know so well seemed to be disappearing. Who else was going to care? *Kendra*. She'd know if I had drawn too many digits. The Mosasaurus joined the Titanosaurus in the trash pile.

I glanced at the clock. It was almost midnight, but I wasn't tired yet. I kept drawing. Every time I looked at what I had drawn, it just ended up in the reject pile. Maybe I was getting delirious but, since nothing I drew seemed any good, I switched gears and stopped trying to draw realistic scenes. Instead, I drew a variety of dinosaurs wearing jerseys and playing a game of soccer. I drew a Velociraptor wearing sunglasses and driving a convertible. I drew dinosaurs with streaked hair and matching outfits dancing on a stage. After all this drawing, I could barely keep my eyes open, so I knew it was time to go to sleep.

I leaned over and threw the papers onto my desk. I finally turned off the flashlight and, for the first time in weeks, fell asleep and dreamed of dinosaurs.

Chapter 33

A NEW PARTNER IN CRIME

I kicked Haji gently under the table. He looked surprised. I very discreetly motioned with my head in the direction of the living room. He squished his eyes together and shrugged his shoulders, not understanding what I wanted. I stared at him impatiently with a look that said, "Do what I say!"

L.B. was playing a word game with Hammy. They did this game every night at dinner. L.B. said a word, like *garden*, and Hammy had to think of a word associated with it. If she said anything remotely related to L.B.'s word, it would count as correct. She gave Hammy a ten-second hug for each ten words she got right. She used my DoodleBoard to keep track. The hug usually lasted longer than ten seconds.

Mom and Dad were watching the proceedings with interest. I knew they were keeping track of how fast Hammy could answer. When Hammy took too long to answer or if her answer was off, I could see them look at each other and I guessed they were ticking off some kind of mental score-card. It was maddening to watch.

"Today's first word is *beach*," L.B. said. She popped four grains of rice into her mouth with her chopsticks. Everybody else had cleaned their plates. Hammy always enjoyed sitting with L.B. as long as she could.

"Oh, good one. Water!" Hammy said. My parents approved of the answer and nodded.

Since everybody else was distracted, Haji and I slipped away.

"What is it, Peter?" he asked when we were in the hall-way far enough away that nobody could hear.

I pulled my notebook out of my pocket. "L.B. and I have a plan," I whispered.

"For what?"

"To help you and Hammy when you move home."

"Peter . . ." Haji's shoulders slumped. "It's hard time. I'm worried. Not sure I can help Hammy by myself . . ."

I frowned at him.

"We heard about this new place in Surrey . . . ," Haji said.

"Not you too!" I whisper-shouted.

"Not a bad idea. They will have Korean-speaking staff and—"

I cut him off. "Look at her, Haji!" I pointed to Hammy. "She's okay! She's not as bad as you think. Let's give her a chance. You can't move her away, not yet!" I tried to stop them, but tears started to well up in my eyes. I rubbed them away angrily and, in the process, scratched my face with the coil of my notebook I was still clutching.

"Peter. You have notebook."

"So?" I said, rubbing the spot on my cheek that I was sure would start bleeding any second.

"You not carry notebook for a long time."

"How do you know?"

"You think I don't notice anything?" he asked. "Why you so angry about moving Hammy to place in Surrey? It might be for the best. Anyway, nothing is for sure yet."

I paused before I answered carefully.

"Because it seems close, but it's not. It seems like we could just stop by anytime, but we won't. Something will stop us. Rush hour traffic or L.B. will have to take one of her classes. It will be something. That thirty-minute drive to see her will feel a lot longer than that. That space between where she is and where we are, it will get bigger and bigger. We need her close. L.B. needs her close. Haji, *I* need her close."

"Peter, she's not going to get better. Doctor told us. Maybe stay stable for a little bit, but soon she will get worse. We don't know when, but we know it will happen."

"I've been reading about it, Haji. I know more than you think I do. You think ripping her away will help? I think it will only make it worse, faster! She won't be near the people who are important to her. Nobody there will care about her the way we care about her. The best way to keep her stable for as long as possible is to have her close to us!"

Haji looked down at the ground and sighed heavily. "What's in your notebook?" he finally asked.

I flipped open the book and started to show him. "L.B. and I have been doing some research."

Chapter 34

SANTA'S LITTLE HELPER

Leaving the daily soccer games proved to be a good decision. I didn't miss them one bit. I didn't even know where my goalie gloves were, and I didn't care. Joe and I spent more time with Samuel and his friends, and when it was raining and we couldn't play basketball, we just stood underneath an awning and talked.

One day when we were just starting to play, Ryan and Liam tried to join our basketball game. "Samuel!" Ryan said.

Samuel turned around with the ball in his hands. "What?" he asked.

"We had a great soccer match on the weekend, didn't we?" Ryan asked.

"Yeah, you scored two goals. Is that what you want me

to tell everyone?" Samuel said to him. He passed the ball and ran up the court.

"Samuel!" Ryan yelled again.

Samuel stopped, looking irritated, and said, "Dude, what do you want?"

"Can Liam and I join your game?" he asked.

"Court's full, man," Samuel replied as he jogged away. "Come back after your shift at the North Pole toy factory is done."

Everyone had been watching their interaction, but I had been watching with greater interest than the others. A few of the guys on the court chuckled a little, but nobody made a big deal about what Samuel said—except Ryan. Ryan flashed Samuel an angry look and then noticed me looking at him.

"What are you staring at, Noodle Boy?" Ryan seethed.

I shrugged my shoulders and tried to suppress a smile. I suddenly liked Samuel more than ever.

FRIDAY, SEPTEMBER 20, 9:05 A.M.
CONDITIONS: THE DAY THE EARTH STOOD STILL

It was first thing Friday morning. The final bell rang and the class was still milling about and getting settled. Ms. Tran stood up in front of the class and was just about to say something when Ryan's hand shot up.

"Yes?" she said.

He waited until everyone was quiet.

"I have some great news!" he said. "I won a writing contest. Look at what I received in the mail yesterday! It's the first of many, I'm sure."

My heart sank.

"The Young Ecologist Society of British Columbia had a writing competition." He lifted up a magazine. "The topic was: how young people can be involved in environmental change. Here's my first-place certificate!"

He smiled broadly and held up the certificate for all to see. Smugness practically leaped off his face.

Environmental change? *That* was his topic? There was a murmur of conversation in the class.

"Doesn't his mom drive one of those huge Escalades?" I heard somebody whisper.

The paper even had a golden star embossed in the bottom-right corner. There was his name in fancy calligraphy under the words "First Place." I wanted to die.

"How wonderful that you are passionate about saving the environment!" Ms. Tran said. "I'm also personally very concerned about the environment and believe that each individual can make positive, meaningful change. For instance, I walk to school once a week instead of driving."

"Oh, I'm no tree hugger," Ryan replied without a shred of humanity on his face. "I wrote it because I could. You don't have to believe in what you're writing to write an argumentative essay. You've just got to be good at arguing."

Ms. Tran's face fell.

"What was the prize?" Stephanie asked, tapping her pencil. "Did you win any money?"

Ryan looked surprised. "The prize is *winning*," he said matter-of-factly.

Stephanie shot him her disgusted look.

"I happen to have brought a copy of my essay to class." Ryan looked hopefully at Ms. Tran.

After an uncomfortable three seconds, Ms. Tran finally said, "Would you care to read it to the class?"

Personally, I would have suggested he start saving the environment by promptly putting his essay in the recycling bin.

"It would be my pleasure!" Ryan reached into his desk. He cleared his throat and stood up. Then he took a swig of water from his single-use water bottle, the kind he brought to school every day, and threw it in the trash. Ms. Tran almost fainted.

Stephanie came up from behind him, picked his bottle out of the trash and put it in the recycling bin, which was sitting right next to the trash bin. She glared at him.

Ryan held his essay between his hands, gave his bangs a flick to the side and he began, "The Earth is in crisis . . ."

I think even Liam groaned.

Chapter 35

DO. OR DO NOT.
THERE IS NO TRY

"I think I want to tidy up my house today," Haji told my mom in the kitchen.

"Oh, sure." Mom wasn't even listening.

"Can Peter help me?" he asked.

"Okay." Mom flipped the page of the newspaper.

"You ready to go?" Haji asked, winking at me quickly.

"I just need a few things." I grabbed my jacket and ran upstairs to gather my supplies.

I tucked my copy of *Fossil Dreams: A Young Scientist's Essential Guide* inside my jacket. I didn't want Mom asking any questions. I had a small plastic bag full of cardstock pieces I had prepared. Those fit easily into my exterior pockets. I made sure I brought a good collection of markers, coloring pencils and black felt-tipped pens.

I hadn't been to Haji and Hammy's house for a few weeks. Haji had been back a couple of times to pick up some more clothes or to get Hammy a book she wanted, but L.B. and I were never invited to go.

As we walked into their house, I closed the door behind me and the *Time* picture slid. "Haji, really, it's time to take this thing down." I gave it its usual adjustment.

"We have more important things to do right now, Peter." He was right.

It took some time for me to feel comfortable, even though I had always considered their house my second home. I stood in the doorway and prepared myself.

I flipped through some of the pages in my notebook just to remind myself what I needed to do. I unloaded my supplies from my jacket pockets and laid them all out on the hallway table.

Haji came up from behind me and put his arm across my shoulders. Pretty soon he wasn't going to be able to do that. Our bodies were moving in opposite directions.

"Ready?" he asked.

I inhaled deeply. "I'm ready."

"Where should we start?"

"The kitchen."

We had put several hours into the kitchen and it was as good as it was ever going to be. My part was done, but Haji still had a few things left he wanted to do. I decided to tackle the rest of the house. I wandered into the living room. I grimaced at the world's ugliest family photo and moved past it. I stopped in front of Hammy's cabinet full of ceramic pigs.

I wondered what happened to the one I'd bought her. I looked for it, but I didn't see it right away, so I started rummaging around the cabinet. Then I noticed there was a thin bottom drawer that I had never really seen before. I gave it a tug and it reluctantly slid open. Loose papers were stacked randomly on top of each other. I picked up the page on the top. It was a sketch of a tall boy wearing a field vest and carrying a shovel. The face was pretty good, but not totally realistic. It was in black ink, with confident lines and short but determined strokes. I could tell it was like a first pass, no corrections, no erasing, no fussing with the lines like you could do in pencil. My hands started shaking.

Haji came into the living room. "Hey, where did you go?" Then he saw what I was holding and I could see his shoulders give way and the corners of his mouth tighten.

"What do you think?" Haji came next to me and peered at the picture.

"Did you do this?"

"No! I can't draw. Hammy did it."

"Hammy?" I was shocked. I didn't know Hammy could draw.

Haji looked disappointed in me. "You didn't know she went to art school?"

"She went to art school?" I didn't mean to shout, but I couldn't help it.

"In Korea. When I met her she was at Ewha Womans University. She was studying fine arts. My friends and I used to sit in a park near her school just to . . ." He looked shy and sly all at once. "You know, look at girls."

"Haji, too much information." I held my hand out like a stop sign.

He chuckled. "She caught my eye. You know how Hammy always take care with her cardigans and scarf? Always like that. Very neat and tidy. So beautiful. All my friends think she was prettiest girl at the university. But Hammy had to quit school after two years because her parents couldn't afford tuition anymore. So, I married her instead." His eyes twinkled from the memories and he smiled.

"She never finished?"

He shook his head.

"Did Hammy regret not being an artist?"

Haji looked surprised. "What do you mean?"

"That she didn't . . . you know, live out her dream?"

"She *did* live out her dream. She had your mom. Hammy was the best mother to her, even though your mom kind of bossy now. We only had one child, so Hammy gave her everything. That's a kind of dream, right? Sometimes dreams can change a little."

"But her art, Haji, what about her art?"

"She does art all the time, in her own way." He gestured to the cabinet full of ceramic pigs. "She looks for art everywhere. The way she decorates the house. It's like her art. Cooking for you, even. When she puts vegetables in a certain way, it's art to her. She never give it up."

How did I not know any of this? How did I not notice? My face flushed.

Haji gave me a minute before he said, "Come on, we have lots of work to do."

I nodded.

"You can take it home. I think Hammy would want you to have it."

I looked down at the picture that Hammy had drawn of me in my field vest. I stared out the kitchen window and caught sight of my abandoned excavation pit. My chest started to hurt.

Chapter 36

UNDER PRESSURE

"L.B.!" Mom shouted up the stairs. "It's time to go see Dr. Stephanova! I couldn't get that green stain out of your lab coat, but it's washed!"

L.B. and I were in my room, trying to ignore each other. She was doing a headstand on her foam mattress while trying to read at the same time. Her braids were splayed on the floor like two dead snakes. I was just sitting on the floor on my bum like a normal human being reading the regular way. Luckily, reading upside down actually required her to concentrate, so she was unusually quiet.

As soon as she heard my mother's voice, she dropped her legs down to the ground and, from her knees, turned around and yelled back down the stairs, "I don't want to go today!"

"I wasn't asking your opinion!" Mom shouted back.

She grabbed Trixie and held him to her ear. "Trixie has a fever!" L.B. shouted.

"Honestly, L.B., stop it! Trixie cannot possibly have a fever—he's a toy dinosaur! Get down here!" Mom's voice was getting louder and more impatient.

"I'll be home in three hours," she said to Trixie as she placed him on her pillow. She tucked him in and pulled up the blanket, so all I could see was his stupid green head poking out. She then got up, left the room and slammed my door behind her. L.B. was forbidden to take Trixie to her mentor sessions. Mom thought it was inappropriate to bring him because, you know, it was in a university class-room and Trixie was, you know, a stuffed dinosaur.

L.B. proceeded to stomp-walk down the hallway and then down the stairs. A stomp-walk is extremely difficult; I've tried it. It involves a lot of anger, tremendous heel strikes to the floor and good speed. When L.B. stomp-walked, she was upset, really upset.

"What's gotten into you?" I heard Mom say as L.B. passed her at the bottom of the stairs.

"When I'm learning about chemical compounds, I am *not* spending time with Hammy! Your priorities are . . . *wrong!*" L.B. spat angrily.

"You see Hammy every single day! She's out for a walk with Haji anyway," Mom exclaimed. "She wouldn't like you to fall behind in your learning."

"What would you know," L.B. grumbled. "Let's get this class over with."

"Peter!" Mom shouted back at me. "Don't forget to do your homework!"

"I'm doing it right now!" I yelled back. I was lying, of course. I was reading a sports magazine I had borrowed from the school library.

"That's what I like to hear!" I heard the front door close.

Finally, some privacy. I had my room to myself for a few hours. And while I should have been enjoying it, looking around, I realized it was a disaster. My desk was a mess. It was usually a lot neater than this, but with L.B. around, the desk just seemed to sprout paper in random places. I put down my magazine and started sorting paper. My sketches. I gathered the whole pile and tossed it straight into the recycling bin.

One page missed the bin and landed on the floor. I picked it up and looked at the picture I'd drawn of Trixie doing dinosaur math. My heart sank. I was just about to throw it in the bin with all the other papers, but just before

I let go of it, I thought of Kendra and the contest. The deadline was in three days. *Three days.*

Part of me wanted to salvage any of the self-respect I had left out there in the badlands and just *try*, take a risk like Joe, or be like Samuel and not live with regret. I took one final long look at the picture of Trixie in my hands. Though it was supposed to be funny and make me laugh, instead it left me feeling depressed. Was this all I could do, some silly picture? I couldn't submit a drawing of my sister's stuffed dinosaur, could I? That would be completely mortifying. Almost as bad as getting an F in the Junior Scientist Dig.

I imagined Kendra opening up my letter, looking at the picture and showing her assistant. "Remember the kid who lasted eighteen minutes in the field during a fossil dig this summer? He actually thinks we might use *this* on the cover!" And the two of them would have a good long laugh about it. I felt a flush rise up from the tips of my toes and burn quickly all the way to my face, like a fuse fueled by humiliation. The feeling exploded out through the top of my head.

Spontaneous human combustion has been reported, but not widely proven by hard science. Would I be the first modern verified case of dying from shame and erupting into

a heap of ash and smoke? No. I would not submit the drawing of Trixie. I'd rather send in *nothing* than something so
lame. I wasn't going to put myself out to Kendra again.
Never again.

What I had known for weeks, but wasn't ready to admit
to myself, finally hit me hard. I had to give up. These little
doodles weren't good enough. I wasn't good enough. Like
removing a bandage, I decided to rip away the idea of sub-
mitting anything to the newsletter in one quick, painful
motion. I was done. I was almost out of time anyway. What
was the point? Trixie doing math went in the bin with all
my other drawings.

Chapter 37

TRUTH TIME

"Is it time, Haji?" I asked, sitting down next to him on the couch after dinner.

"I think this weekend would be a good time," he said confidently.

"Do you think we did enough?"

"We did everything we could."

"Do you think it's going to help?"

"Peter, you did a good job." He patted my knee.

I wasn't sure about that. I needed to observe the effects of my work in real life. Sometimes things sound good in theory but, in reality, they don't work. That's why scientists have to do trials and experiments. You just never know if what you *think* will work, actually will. The doubt was killing me. But I'd have to wait a few more days to find out.

SATURDAY, OCTOBER 5, 7:40 A.M.

CONDITIONS: TREMORS (MY GUTS, NOT THE
EARTH'S MANTLE)

Haji stood up at breakfast. He dinged the side of his water glass with his fork. "Everyone, everyone. Listen, please."

My heart started racing. This was it.

"I'd like for everybody to come to my house today," Haji said.

Mom glared at him suspiciously. "Do you need to pick up something?"

"No, Peter and I want to show you something."

L.B. buried her face into the sleeve of Hammy's cardigan and started giggling. "The suspense is too much to bear!"

"What's going on?" Dad asked. "Peter? Haji?"

"Let's go," Haji said impatiently.

"So early!" Hammy said as she strained to look at the clock. She was understandably confused. "What time is it, L.B.? I can't read the clock."

"It's 7:40."

"What's so important to see at 7:40 on a Saturday morning?" Mom quizzed Haji.

"*Cha*, stop asking questions and get dressed!"

"But L.B. hasn't finished her breakfast!" Mom protested.

"Bring it in the car! Come! Come!" Haji gathered everybody up.

"But I need my sweater," Hammy said.

"*Yobo*, you're wearing a sweater already," Haji said gently.

Hammy looked down, patted her chest and shook her head. "Ah, I forgot."

I knew Mom and Dad had just added that to their mental checklist of reasons why Hammy needed to move out of her house. The thought left me petrified. I was sitting there like a zombie statue.

Haji tugged me by my armpit and urged me to stand. He whispered, "Don't be nervous!"

"Too bad. I am!" I whispered back.

L.B. leaned in and said quietly, "I have complete confidence that you executed our plan to perfection." She then started giggling again. She even started to spin around in circles like a top gone out of control.

"Okay, what in the world is happening?" Mom shouted. "I am not going anywhere until I get some more information." She crossed her arms.

Haji said angrily, "This is not about you. Not everything about you. Just drive the minivan, okay?"

"What is going on?" Mom asked again as she walked through the door at Hammy and Haji's house.

Haji adjusted the *Time* picture before he said, "Peter did a lot of work."

"You helped me a lot, Haji." We smiled at each other.

"Come inside, look! Look!" Haji motioned for everybody to come inside. Everybody was so tentative, especially Hammy.

Hammy didn't seem to know where to go first. "Let's start here," I suggested. I guided her by the elbow into the kitchen. I held on lightly because she had just had her cast removed and her arm was weak.

I glanced over at Mom, who had had a slightly suspicious look on her face from the moment we left our house, but her face had relaxed and she was taking it all in.

Hammy and I stopped and stood in the doorway of the kitchen. Each cabinet and drawer had been streamlined and excess stuff removed, and each front had a label on it. Haji and I had made each label by hand. I was nervous about what she was going to say about me and Haji rearranging her kitchen.

"Oh!" Hammy laughed. "A label for kimchi jars!" She pointed. It was my favorite picture. I had used up all the ink in my orange marker for that one.

"Look here! The chopstick drawer!" L.B. said.

"You have a lot of chopsticks, Hammy," I told her.

"Every Korean person have lots of chopsticks," she said, chuckling.

I watched Hammy look at each label carefully. I chewed my lip wondering if I'd made the right choices. I had decided that there was no single size of label that would work. Each drawer and cabinet had a hand-drawn picture of its interior contents. I wanted the pictures to be big enough but not overwhelming. I wanted them to be realistic and colored accurately. The kitchen took a long time. I was glad to have Haji with me the whole time because when I was coloring, my hand started to cramp and he helped me when he could.

Each label was also bilingual. I wrote in English and Haji wrote the Korean translation. Haji and I both noticed that Hammy was flipping in and out of Korean and English a lot more than she used to, so we thought she needed both. He also had very neat printing, just like me. I loved watching him draw the Korean characters, each word looking like its own little piece of art.

"This is so good, Peter." Hammy beamed at me as she ran her hand across the front of a label.

"It was L.B.'s idea," I said, giving her credit. "She found this really great article with practical advice to help when . . ." I struggled to find the words. "When somebody really important to you needs help."

L.B. smiled proudly and she hugged Hammy's waist.

"Wow," Hammy said as she opened a drawer and looked carefully inside. "So organized." She hadn't been home in so long I wondered if she recognized anything. I wondered if any of this would help.

I watched Hammy closely. It looked like she was seeing this kitchen for the first time.

"Peter!" Mom said to me quietly. "This is incredible."

I smiled awkwardly.

"It's supposed to help a lot," I said. "So she doesn't feel confused. And if she's looking for something, she can just read the label instead of randomly opening drawers and cupboards. The kitchen and the bathroom were the hardest to do. There's just so much important stuff hidden away."

Dad patted my back. "Where did you learn to do all *this?*" he asked as he looked around in wonder.

I thought about it. The answer was so obvious.

"Paleontology," I answered quietly. But they weren't waiting for an answer, and they had gone off to wander around and look at the labels and the way I had organized things.

I didn't realize it until that very moment, and the realization hit me hard. All that time I had spent reading books, digging in the backyard pit and making field notes, none of that was wasted time. It had all brought us here to this moment where, at last, it was my turn to take care of Hammy.

"Did you see Peter's maps?" Haji asked Dad.

"No! Show me!"

Haji showed him the one I had posted at the bottom of the stairs. I drew that one in two ways: bird's-eye view, like a flat, two-dimensional floor plan, and a three-dimensional picture—so if Hammy stood in the living room, she could look at the map and see that up the stairs to the left there were bedrooms. I also drew a very prominent arrow in the hallway pointing to the washroom.

When Mom was alone in the kitchen looking at the labels on the cabinet fronts, I walked up to her and asked, "Do you think she'll be able to stay at home now?"

"What do you mean?"

"You won't send her away to a seniors' home?" I said. "Not even that place in Surrey?"

Mom sighed heavily. "Peter, how did you find out?"

"Partly the recycling, partly I overheard you."

Mom closed her eyes.

"Listen, Peter, I don't know how Hammy is going to do at home. Nobody knows how this will play out over time. Dementia is very common in the elderly, and for some people it progresses quickly and for other people it doesn't. We have to keep our options open," Mom said gently. "She is on several waiting lists right now. But I promise you we will give her every opportunity to stay at home, as long as it makes sense for everyone. We hired an aide to come visit her twice a week and help with cleaning, and, of course, we will be visiting more often too. We'll have to wait and see."

I looked down to the ground.

"Peter, what you did here, to help Hammy, I'm sure that it is going to help her right now. It's going to make her life here, right now, so much easier. That's pretty amazing, right? Isn't that all we can ask for, to enjoy the here and now?" she asked hopefully.

I nodded and didn't speak right away. I wanted to make sure Mom knew I was listening. "L.B. will be crushed if Hammy gets sent away," I said. I should have also included myself, but I didn't.

"I know," Mom said. "Then let's enjoy being together for as long as we can."

Chapter 38

WHEN MOM DOESN'T KNOW BEST

FRIDAY, NOVEMBER 8, 8:30 A.M.

CONDITIONS: CRISP. SEASON IS DEFINITELY

CHANGING

The best thing education has given children is the extra-long weekend. I don't know what teachers do exactly on "professional development days," but based on what I've seen in the staff room on regular school days, there is probably cake. And when there's a PD day on a Friday and then a holiday on the following Monday, in this case Remembrance Day, well, those four days off are pretty sweet for the kids too, even if we don't have cake.

The first day of a four-day long weekend break from school is a bit disorienting because it's a Friday but it has that Saturday feel. There was no rush to get out the door and no reason to change out of my pajamas.

Mom was really going all out this morning—she was making poached eggs, on a weekday! She was whisking the hollandaise sauce vigorously when the doorbell rang.

"Peter, I can't stop or the sauce will break. Can you see who it is?" Her wrist flew around in circles.

"Sure." My pj's weren't super embarrassing this morning, just old sweatpants and a T-shirt. Both were just a little too small.

I cracked the front door open. At first all I could see was a bright pink sweater. It was Hammy. I opened the door wider.

"Hammy!" I proclaimed. "Haji!" He was standing right behind her.

"Good morning!" They stepped into the house.

"Mom? Dad?" Mom yelled from the kitchen. "What's wrong?"

"Just stopping by," Hammy said reassuringly.

L.B. raced down the stairs and ran into Hammy's arms.

"I was just thinking about you!" L.B. gushed.

"Do you want some eggs?" Mom asked.

"Sure!" Hammy and Haji sat down at the table.

Mom gave everybody their breakfasts. It may have been the best meal she'd ever made. L.B., the notorious nibbler, licked her plate clean like a cat. Hammy even asked for more ham, which made Mom happy.

Hammy and Haji had been back in their house for about two weeks now and everybody was adjusting. It was a bittersweet day when they packed up their things from our place. Haji and I had done what we could to make it easy for Hammy to feel good in her house, and after all those weeks sleeping next to L.B., I was ready to get my bed back and her out of my room. Sitting around eating breakfast with them again, I realized I missed them a lot.

"I found circus camp," Hammy said to Mom as she took her last bite and put down her fork.

"You're a little too old to run away and join the circus, Mom," she said humorlessly.

"Not for me," Hammy replied irritably. "For L.B. It's only for four days over the long weekend."

Mom stopped loading the dishwasher and looked at Hammy, confused. After finishing her breakfast, L.B. had left the table to read *Human Invention: A History* on the sofa. Now she looked up hopefully and put her book down.

"What do you mean?" Mom asked.

"I google it," Hammy replied.

"How do you know how to use Google?" Mom couldn't hide her shock.

"Occupational therapist teach me to use it for memory games. I have many apps now. They have one spot left yesterday, so I took it," Hammy said. She glanced at her watch. "It starts in thirty minutes."

"I don't know about this. L.B.'s schedule is far too busy for circus camp," Mom replied. "It's not exactly *enriching* either, is it, Mom?"

Hammy looked annoyed. She pointed to L.B.'s large calendar of extracurricular activities. "Her other class has break right now—it's long weekend! She's not busy! I paid already anyway. I take her!"

Mom looked over at L.B. and said, as if Hammy wasn't even there, "Sorry, L.B., Hammy doesn't know what you like. I'll try to cancel it."

Hammy looked angry. I felt angry too. It felt like Mom was treating Hammy like a child. I was offended for Hammy.

"Don't you dare!" L.B. shouted, leaping to her feet. "I'm going to circus camp! Hammy knows me just fine, even better than you!"

"Circus camp is not important!" Mom said.

"Life not only textbooks, you know." Hammy took a deep breath and stared Mom down. "You never see her. But I see her," Hammy said seriously.

"Come, L.B." Hammy stuck out her hand. "Let's go."

Hammy tapped Haji's shoulder and motioned with her head that it was time for them to leave. He put down the newspaper and reached for his jacket. He dug around his pocket for his keys and turned to look at Mom. He shrugged his shoulders. "Thanks for the eggs." Gently, he put his hand on her shoulder and gave it a squeeze as his keys jingled in his hand.

L.B. ran to the door with Trixie tucked under her arm, grabbed Hammy's hand and didn't look back.

Mom stood there with her mouth open. I pulled out my notebook from my pocket and quietly turned the pages. I wrote:

HAMMY IS HAVING A REALLY GOOD DAY. =)

Chapter 39

THIS ASIAN WHIZ KID

L.B. had been going off with Hammy and Haji to circus camp all weekend. The first night, she came home and spent the three hours before dinner flinging herself around the backyard, even though it was dark and the grass was wet and cold.

The camp lent her a unicycle to take home the next day, and in the late afternoon, you could hear her screaming, "Forward! Steady! Reverse!" as she practiced pedaling up and down the sidewalk. I had to put on headphones and watch YouTube videos featuring the greatest dunks in basketball history to block out the noise.

On the last day of the camp, when he picked L.B. up in the morning, Haji said to my mom, "I pick Peter up with

L.B. at the end of the day. We have special grandparent and grandchild dinner, okay? You two have date-night time tonight!" Haji winked at her.

"Are you sure?" she asked.

"No problem. Hammy and I take care of everything," he said confidently. "She's feeling very good today, lots of energy. You have helped a lot lately. You take a rest."

Out of the corner of my eye, I caught L.B. giving him a thumbs-up and thought that that was a bit weird.

I looked back at Mom to see what she would say. She did need a break. She hadn't asked me to do extra math for a really long time, so I knew she was very preoccupied.

"Sounds good," she said as she smiled at Haji. I could see her relax.

"Peter, I come back here around three thirty, okay?" Haji said.

"Sure." We had never had a special grandparent-grandchild night before.

3:45 P.M.

When they picked me up as planned, L.B. was already in the car, having just finished circus camp. She smelled like old gym socks and her hair stuck to her forehead from dried sweat. I scrunched my nose and tried to breathe through my mouth, but sometimes that made my throat dry. I patted my pocket for my inhaler and I opened the window for a bit of fresh air. I looked at the space between us and noticed Trixie was smashed into the cupholder of L.B.'s car seat.

As we approached Hammy and Haji's house, L.B. started to giggle. I looked over at her.

"What's so funny?" I asked.

She put her hand up to her mouth to try to suppress her laughter, but she couldn't. She just kept giggling. Her body started to shake and convulse, and it almost looked like she was having a seizure, but she looked too happy to be having a medical emergency.

Then Hammy and Haji started to laugh.

"What is so funny?" I asked again, louder.

L.B. picked up Trixie and shoved him in front of her mouth so she was laughing into him.

"Oh, it's nothing," Haji said, trying to dismiss all the laughter. He wiped a tear from his eye, and Hammy fanned herself with her hand.

My face started to turn red. I felt like I was the only one who didn't get the joke. We pulled up in front of Hammy and Haji's house.

"Go!" L.B. said, motioning with her hand for Hammy and Haji to exit the car.

When she got out of the car, L.B. started to do little stationary hops, shifting from one foot to the other like an excited penguin.

They walked toward the front door. I lagged behind, still wondering what everybody had thought was so funny. They all seemed so weird. Haji looked over his shoulder before unlocking the front door. He pushed it open, but nobody went inside.

"Go first," Hammy said to me.

"Why?" I asked suspiciously.

"Just do what Hammy says!" She waved me inside.

I stepped inside cautiously, wondering if they had a big practical joke planned, and then I kicked off my shoes. I let them all come in behind me, but they seemed to want to huddle near the door. I looked around, waiting for an evil clown or a *Star Wars* stormtrooper to jump out and scare me. Haji finally closed the front door.

Automatically I reached over to the wall, ready to straighten the *Time* "Asian-American Whiz Kids" picture. But something was different. It wasn't there anymore. There was something new there instead. My arm fell to my side and I took a step toward the new picture to have a good hard look.

It was the cover of a Royal Tyrrell newsletter that I had never seen before. On the cover was *my* picture. One of the ones I had forgotten about and assumed was in the pile I'd thrown into the recycling bin. But here it was, right there in the frame, on the cover of the newsletter. In the bottom-right corner it said, *"K-Pop Dino* by Peter Lee, age eleven, Vancouver, B.C."* I unexpectedly realized that it kind of looked like Samuel, but as a dinosaur, wearing his diamond earring, athleisure clothes and with a head of streaked hair.

THE ROYAL TYRELL MUSEUM

MEMBER NEWSLETTER   •   ISSUE NO. XI

"K-Pop Dino" by Peter Lee, Age 11, Vancouver, BC

I looked at Haji, Hammy and L.B. They all had big smiles. "How? What? But!" I couldn't get out words as I pointed dumbly to the newsletter.

"Your little sister very tricky, Peter!" Haji said. "She told me about contest. L.B. showed me newsletter. It was her idea to send in picture. We all like this one."

I was stunned into silence.

"Who knew you could draw dinosaur looking so Korean? Very impressive!" Haji said as he put his hand on my shoulder.

I looked at L.B., who was smiling nervously.

"She gave me envelope with picture and told me, 'Haji, you must do overnight express shipping or we don't make the deadline!'" Haji continued.

"I included a note to Kendra," L.B. said. "I hope you're not mad that I misrepresented myself as you."

"When did you find this picture?"

"I noticed things. I observed."

I stared at her skeptically.

"Okay, I rummaged around your desk," she admitted. "I selected this one because it was by far the most original. I was worried you were just going to let the deadline pass. The dinosaur herd trampling a young boy playing soccer was an excellent drawing, but far too violent. Here's an extra copy of the newsletter. They're not out yet. Kendra sent it to us early. Are you mad?" She looked worried.

I reached for the newsletter. My fingers touched my drawing. I needed to check the articles. I needed to know.

I flipped through it, quickly but thoroughly.

"What are you looking for, Peter?" L.B. asked.

My eyes and fingers raced through the pages of the newsletter until the last page. Then I flipped the last page shut and declared, "That barf-bag Ryan's article did *not* make the issue! Hammy! It's ice cream time! Do you have ice cream?"

"Better," she said. "I bought red bean buns!"

"That's not what I had in mind, but I don't care! Red bean buns for everyone!" I yelled.

Hammy went to the kitchen to get the celebratory dessert.

I looked over at L.B. and, as softly and as gently as I could, I said, "Thank you, L.B. I'd given up on the idea. I didn't think anything I drew was good enough."

She whispered, "Sometimes you need others to believe in you before you can believe in yourself. I've always known you had long, talented limbs. Maybe now you know it too."

I held the copy of the newsletter in my hands and

brought it up to my chest. I was shaking. I patted my pocket and felt my inhaler.

"Here you go!" Hammy said as she brought out a plate of buns. "My famous grandson gets to pick first!"

I felt my cheeks flush. As I ate my red bean bun, I looked around their living room and kitchen and saw all the work that Haji and I had done labeling their house. I was ready to accept the fact that I was good at organizing and planning. I could draw maps and be methodical when I wanted to be. Look at the results! It had really helped Hammy out. As she'd prepared to bring our desserts out, I'd seen her reading the labels on the cabinets, so I knew they were helping her.

I don't know, maybe paleontology and I weren't *quite* done with each other yet. At first, I thought paleontology was studying dinosaur taxonomy and evolution and the act of locating and retrieving fossilized specimens. But the more I thought about it, I realized that it was more. It was *so* much more. It was learning how to learn. It was learning to approach problems in an orderly way. It was record keeping. It was observing the environment. It was gathering information and piecing together a conclusion.

I don't know how long our solution was going to keep Hammy at home, but at least she was *home*. And I had helped it all happen by using skills I had developed because of an obsessive, dorky love of paleontology. Plan, observe, organize, record and execute. I guess it helped that I was pretty good at drawing too. I got that from Hammy.

Haji sat down beside me and put his hand on my knee. He whispered, "Hammy is very happy about your drawings and labels. She uses them very much. Have you seen her?"

"Yeah, I have." I smiled.

"Sometimes I think she can't find something, but before I offer to help, I let her look. When she finds something herself, I think it makes her feel proud, like she can do it by herself."

"It's going to make her feel better if she can do things without asking for help all the time," I told him, keeping my voice low.

"I think you have many good talents and artistic, but scientific brain. Rare combination. I have my own whiz *grand*kids right here all this time. I don't need that *Time* anymore. I'm happy it's gone." He gave my knee a final tap.

I was glad I hadn't thrown out my bags and boxes of dinosaur stuff yet. It was all still where I had last shoved it, in the back of my closet. It was out of sight, but it was no longer out of mind. I wondered if the Royal Tyrrell Museum had any paleontology programs for children that took place *inside*, where it wasn't so hot and dusty. There must be a whole branch of paleontology besides outdoor fieldwork that I hadn't ever considered. I'd have to do some more research. Maybe I'd even give outdoor fieldwork one more try, who knows.

I took a bite of red bean bun and I sighed happily. Then I looked up and saw the world's ugliest family photo sitting on top of my grandparents' piano, and instead of it bothering me, I just laughed.

"So, what are we having for special grandparent-grandchild dinner?" I asked as my stomach rumbled. That red bean bun was good, but I was going to need more to eat.

Hammy and Haji looked at each other. They seemed to have forgotten about the *dinner* portion of our special grandparent-grandchild dinner.

"Korean restaurant?" Haji asked.

"Korean restaurant," we all agreed.

After dinner, before L.B. and I got out of Hammy and Haji's car, Hammy turned around and said to us, "I know I'm getting old and my memory has problems. But you two make Hammy feel so happy. I never want to forget this weekend and how happy I feel when I see L.B. jumping and tumbling and leaping at circus camp. And then when we opened envelope to see Peter's drawing. Oh! Hammy couldn't ask for more. Even if Hammy forgets, I want *you* to remember."

"*Salanghaeyo*," L.B. said to Hammy.

"*Nado neoleul salanghae*," Hammy said as she reached out for L.B.'s hand. I didn't need to speak Korean to understand.

Then Hammy reached for my hand. "I love you too, Peter." I held her hand tightly in mine.

Before I got out of the car, Hammy said, "Oh! I almost forgot." She rummaged around her purse. "I found this for you. It's antique."

She passed me a ceramic figure of a Triceratops. The green paint was worn around its neck, as if it had been held a lot, and one of the horns was missing. It was perfect.

"Thank you, Hammy." I held the Triceratops gently in my hand. "You always know what I like."

When we got back inside the house, I showed my parents the newsletter cover. "Look at this," I said bashfully.

They looked pleased and both said, "Wow!"

"*You* drew this?" Mom looked shocked.

Before they could say anything more, I said, "Mom, Dad. Do you think we could get a new family photo, but include Hammy and Haji this time? We could give them a copy of the photo and I could label who everybody is, so she doesn't forget us? I'll try really hard not to blink."

"Peter," Dad said warmly, "that is a great idea."

"I agree!" Mom said, smiling with shining eyes. "I think Hammy would really like that."

"Petey," L.B. gushed. "It's a perfect idea." She hugged Trixie tight.

"Can we *not* go back to the Vietnamese sandwich shop that pretends it's a photography studio?" I asked.

"But Minh does make good sandwiches," Dad joked.

Everybody laughed. Then L.B. launched herself onto my back, but this time, I was ready for her and I let her hang off me for a while. She snuggled her chin into my shoulder.

"Can Trixie be in this one?" L.B. asked.

I saw my mother frown.

"Admit it, Mom," I said. "Trixie is part of the family!"

She sighed heavily, because she knew I was right.

Later, when I went upstairs, I looked at the picture that Hammy had drawn of me in my field vest. I ran my fingertips over the black ink before I taped it to the back of my door. I pulled my notebook out of my pocket and sat down on my bed. I pushed the pencil out of the coil and closed my eyes to think about what I wanted to draw. Of course I knew.

I wrote "My Family" across the top of the page and started drawing. It wasn't a great sketch, but I drew myself in the middle. As the tallest person in the family, I obviously belonged in the center, and then I drew everybody else around me: Mom with her awkward smile; Dad *without* dandruff flakes on his glasses; L.B. with her hair in a braid, clutching Trixie; Haji with his pants pulled up a little too high; and finally Hammy wearing her signature cardigan and scarf combination. I hoped that this was how we would be for a long time. But I knew that things were going to change. And when they did, this is how I wanted to remember us.

MY FAMILY

ACKNOWLEDGMENTS

The inspiration for this story came from a dinosaur plush toy that I had purchased for my daughter on our trip to Drumheller in 2011. He became "Bracha" because even though she was a very verbal two-year-old, "Brachiosaurus" is a mouthful. She clutched that dinosaur constantly and he came with us everywhere. Until one day, after carrying him around for almost two years, he could not be found. We had had lunch at a dim sum restaurant in Richmond, B.C., and then gone for ice cream at the DQ next door. I called both places and asked if they had found a stuffed green dinosaur. They both replied no. We drove back to check ourselves. My daughter sat in the back of the car, seemingly nonplussed. I was a mess. What would she do without Bracha?

Both the restaurant and the DQ showed no signs of Bracha. I even checked the garbage. He was gone. The next day, I called the Royal Tyrrell Museum's gift shop and explained my situation. They asked for a picture, which of course I had, since he had been with us everywhere every day for the past two years. They kindly informed me that they could send a replacement. I told them, "I'll pay for express shipping!"

Still reeling from the loss of Bracha, we kept busy and cleaned the house. I opened the drawer of the coffee table to organize all the various objects little kids collect. Guess who was sitting in the drawer? It was Bracha! He was never lost! He had just been stuffed inside the drawer of the coffee table all this time. My daughter claimed to not know how he got there. Small children are very unreliable sources of information. Utterly relieved (I believe I even cried), I decided that she was no longer allowed to carry Bracha outside of the house.

When the package from the Royal Tyrrell museum arrived the following day, I shoved it, unopened, in the kitchen cabinet above the microwave. Backup Bracha was no longer needed and stayed in the cabinet for a few years until we renovated our kitchen. At this point, she was still attached to Bracha, but the strong bond had faded.

Packing up the cupboards to prepare for the renovation, I found the package from the museum. I was curious about long-forgotten Backup Bracha, and as I was about to open the package, my kids saw what I was doing. I explained the whole story. We pulled a fresh, bright, clean dinosaur out of the bubble wrapping and marvelled at how different this stuffed dinosaur looked from old Bracha, who had done a lot of living and had endured many cycles in the washing machine. Then we looked at the tag.

We all burst out laughing. Turns out Bracha was actually an Apatosaurus. To this day, I don't know why we always assumed Bracha was supposed to be a Brachiosaurus. We named Backup Bracha "Appa." Obviously.

Bracha and Appa now sit together on a bench in my daughter's room. Little do they know that they were the inspiration for this story about the Lee family.

This story started off as a short little road trip story, less than half the book you are currently holding in your hands. I had a lot of help getting it to this stage.

To Mike, Alice and Hilary. Thank you for all the early feedback. Brainstorming with you helped shape the story, and while I got to keep a lot of the fun bits, you helped me add the more substantive ideas. I always had the quirk, but you helped me find the heart. I am grateful.

To my young beta readers, Emerson and Augustine. Your feedback was amazing and so helpful. I remain impressed with your ability to critique and commend at the same time. (I know you're Lees too, but that's just a coincidence.)

To my agent, Laurel Symonds, who picked up this story from her slush pile. Thank you for constant support and your thoughtful and incredible editing ideas. She must also be applauded for putting up with my terrible proofreading and archaic keyboarding habits.

To my editor, Lynne Missen, who scooped up this little story quicker than I could have ever hoped for because she got it. I am still not sure how she can read a story with such insight and attention to detail, but it is truly a gift to have an editor who asks all the right questions. Seriously, how do you do it? Thank you to the team at Tundra/Penguin Random House Canada for loving my story as much as I do.

To my copy editor, Kelly Jones. Nothing gets by you. I mean nothing. I am in awe of your talent (and quite frankly, a little bit afraid).

To my fellow Electric Eighteen, Sophie Gonzalez, who so kindly offered to read the story on very, very short notice. She gave me important insights on living with asthma. Also Diane Magras for taking the time to read and provide comments. The community of writers I have found in my very brief life as an author has been amazing, supportive and generous.

To my family. Thanks for trying to leave me alone when I'm sitting at my computer. But I get it, that dinner isn't going to miraculously cook itself, is it?

For all the beautiful and charming art, please join me in celebrating the artist, Julie Kwon. You put my story and characters to illustration in a way that still blows my mind. You are so talented. Thank you.

While I have been to the Royal Tyrrell Museum (twice!), the contents of this story are fiction and a product of my imagination. I thank the museum for kindly sending me Backup Bracha all those years ago and providing me with inspiration for the site of Peter's personal failures and potential future triumphs. I hope you don't get too many kids asking you when the next Junior Scientist Dig will be scheduled.

Also, if you've never seen the Kukkiwon Demonstration Team give a taekwondo performance, what are you waiting for? You will cheer louder than L.B., I promise.